APOCALYPSE FALL

APOCALYPSE FALL

Tyler H. Jolley

Mary H. Geis

JOLLEY CHRONICLES

For my parents who let me grow up in the 80's.

CHAPTER 1

Matt Voorhees stared out the largest picture window in the main cabin of Camp New Beginnings. Outside was a picturesque winter wonderland worthy of a tacky gilded frame placed above an afghan-covered couch. If only he had a couch, and a home, and parents.

Well, technically, he *did* have parents. They were just cryogenically frozen inside a cave—somewhere. And hopefully still alive.

"Is the snow ever going to let up?" Matt crossed his arms over the *Commodore 64* logo on his shirt. The roaring fireplace was nice, but it only really kept them warm if they were close. "This is getting ridiculous. It's probably snowed another foot."

"Better, like, watch out, Victoria," Kim said. "Much more snow, and it'll be deeper than you are tall."

"Very funny." Victoria stood with pin-straight posture and smoothed her long, black Gothic dress. "I'm not that short." She looked down at her shoes, away from Kim's judging glare.

"Chill out," Stacy said. "Besides, we have a bunch of buff guys here who can carry you—if the snow ever stops."

"I can manage myself," Victoria said. "Catherine, will you French braid my hair?"

"You should tease it up like Elvira and plop it on top of your head like this." Stacy gathered her frizzy, strawberry-blond curls on top of her head. "It'll give you a few inches."

"Come on." Catherine motioned with her chin toward the hearth. "Let's do it over here. You know, I've never had my hair braided. It's too thick and curly."

"I can try after you do mine," Victoria said.

Catherine waddled toward the fireplace, holding up an oversized pair of gray sweatpants over her striped shorts. Most had just opted to use blankets, but a few layered on what they could find in the tattered trunk of old clothes. Once they were closer to the crackling flames, Matt couldn't hear their conversation, but Victoria's shoulders relaxed, and a small smile crept onto her pale face.

Cody sidled up to Matt and pressed his forehead against the window, leaving a greasy smudge.

"First time I saw snow in Texas, I thought it was neato burrito," Cody said. "Now it's the ugliest thing I ever done seen."

"No joke," Matt said. "It's so frustrating. We're stuck. Mother Nature wins again."

"How you feelin'?" Cody turned to Darin.

"I just needed a day to get myself right." Darin shifted

in his folding chair. "I'm still not a hundred percent, but I'm getting there."

"Good. I'm glad." Matt stared back out at the flat gray sky, willing the non-existent sun to shine.

The only shirt large enough to fit Darin was a navy-blue polo with the word "Counselor" embroidered onto the left breast and a pair of too-short, pleated khaki shorts. Matt found a small bit of comfort in the counselor shirt. It seemed to tell everyone that Darin was in charge, and it took the pressure off him.

"Wh-what's the plan?" Nathan asked. He had a blanket slung over his shoulders. Only the *AS* was visible on his NASA shirt.

"I guess as soon as it stops snowing, we go," Matt said.

"No, not th-th-that." Nathan shifted his gaze to the floor. "The bodies."

"Right." Matt pinched the bridge of his nose. "Justin, you said you saw the bodies in the flood water?"

"What's that, chief?" Justin cupped his ear but made no attempt to come closer to Matt.

Matt walked toward Justin, Rhett, Stacy, and Kim. Cody, Nathan, and Darin followed behind him.

"You said you saw Dr. Westbrook and the girl, um, float by?" Matt asked.

"Yep." Justin shuffled a deck of cards. "They were pretty bloated too. Good job on burying them, Nathan."

"I'm so-sorry," Nathan said.

"Nah, I'm just giving you a hard time," Justin said. "I wasn't exaggerating, though. They're pretty messed up."

"Sick!" Kim said. "That's, like, totally disgusting,

and I won't listen to this. Come on, Rhett. Bring me a sleeping bag or something."

Kim turned on a heel. The pleats on her cheerleading skirt flashed yellow and white. Rhett shrugged and followed her toward the theater stage.

"We'll need to bury Kyle too. Pay our respects, you know." Cody gripped the spot where a rodeo belt buckle should have been and nodded at Matt.

"Yes, we'll do that first. Before we go to the mountain," Matt said.

"I thought you were in a big hurry," Darin said. "I'm not complaining, just saying."

"I'd like to get them buried before they . . . I can't even believe I'm saying this, but we probably should do it before they thaw out," Matt said.

"Th-three graves is a l-lot of work," Nathan said. "And we have to go deeper this time."

"Yes," Matt said. "All hands on deck this time."

"Or we could just do one big hole," Justin said.

"What?" Stacy gasped. "That's uncivilized."

"For once, I agree with you, Justin," Matt said.

"It does seem a little, I dunno, disrespectful," Cody said.

"Well, cowboy, we're fresh out of coffins and backhoes," Justin said.

"I agree," Darin said. "You guys can put it to a vote if you'd like."

"No," Matt said. "It's not ideal, but it has to get done, and done quickly. They're rotting—we have no time to waste."

"Then it's settled," Justin said. "Pop a squat, let's play poker."

A loud gust of wind rattled the door. Matt secretly hoped it was someone coming to rescue them, but he knew better. This was up to them.

* * *

Neither Matt nor Darin was in the mood to play cards. Plus, Justin was on Matt's side at the moment. He didn't want to sully the relationship by whipping him at poker. The large gym had finally started to warm up. The fireplace was big, but the room was bigger. He passed by Kim and Rhett on the stage. They lay facing each other, with their legs intertwined. Kim brushed a lock of Rhett's blond hair off his forehead. They looked like dirt-covered Ken and Barbie dolls. Only this Ken doll was 6'6", with big blue eyes and a big, dumb brain. Kim whispered into Rhett's ear, and he laughed, then responded by tickling her.

"You think they ever get tired of playing tonsil hockey?" Matt asked, pointing his thumb toward them.

"Have they been like this the whole time?" Darin asked, hoisting himself onto the stage next to Matt.

"Before, actually. They woke up on the bus ride to the cryovault. They say they didn't see anything because they were too busy doing that." He pointed at them.

"Wait, are we sure they didn't see anything?" Darin asked. "Maybe they know where the vault is."

"We asked them a few times," Matt said. "Trust me,

we got more relationship details than I cared to hear, but nothing useful. Ah, here we are."

Matt did his best Vanna White impression and presented the tapes to Darin. Eighteen black rectangular halves and the spools lay splayed out on a *Gremlins* beach towel. Small screws and three screwdrivers lay amongst the organized chaos.

"I hope these still work," Matt said.

"Me too," Darin said. "Good idea on taking them apart to dry out."

"Thanks. I accidentally spilled water on my mom's new Neil Diamond cassette once and used this same method to dry it out. The case cracked a little, but it still worked." Matt tightened the tape on the reels, then carefully placed the back piece over it. "Hand me a Phillips, will ya? I like the orange-handled one best."

"Trav's Auto Care." Darin examined the screwdriver and his face darkened. "I'm here. Alive and breathing. Whoever this Trav was, he isn't. Gone. Dead. Like everyone else in the world. It's kind of surreal when you think about it."

"Yeah." Matt took the tool from Darin and slowly replaced the screws. "It makes me wonder how and why we were picked."

"Me too," Darin said, bowing his head. "Me too."

"You know, with all the snow, it's too bad we can't go sledding," Matt said, changing the subject.

"I haven't been sledding since I was a kid." Darin laughed. "We could use the canoe."

"My parents drove me to Tahoe a few times with our

dog. He was a Chesapeake Bay Retriever. You know what they look like?"

"No. I'm not a big fan of dogs," Darin said.

"What? How is that even possible? Dogs truly are a man's best friend."

"Not when they're chasing you," Darin said. "I used to deliver papers."

"A paperboy?" Matt laughed.

"Hey, I was only twelve when I was frozen, remember? Anyway, a few would chase me relentlessly. I got bitten once. It scared me."

Statements like that were odd to Matt. Darin had been put in cryosleep just like them, but he'd been awakened for nearly a decade before he was forced back to sleep. Actual time had passed for him. He'd aged. Somehow getting older than Matt, despite being born five years after him.

"Saber wouldn't have done that," Matt said.

"You named your dog Saber?"

"Yep." Matt beamed. "I love movies. *Star Wars* is one of my favorites. Anyway, Saber loved the snow. I grew up in Nevada, so we had to drive to the mountains to see snow. Saber would ride on the sled with me, all eighty pounds of him. We'd fly down those hills. It's one of my favorite memories."

Matt's voice cracked, and his eyes filled with tears. He turned away from Darin and wiped his eyes.

"You really liked that dog, huh?" Darin asked.

"It's not that." Matt cleared his throat. "It's everything. I need to make sure my family is okay. And after that, I want to rebuild. Have a dog again. Live normal.

Not eat expired canned food. And none of that can happen while the sky vomits snow all over us."

"I know," Darin said. "We all do. Well, maybe not those two." He pointed to Rhett and Kim. "They're about three seconds away from actually *showing* us how babies are made. Hey! You two cover up or get a room!"

Matt laughed and dried his eyes one more time. "I think this tape will work." He used his index finger to spin the reels. "Cody, can you fire up the gennie?"

CHAPTER 2

Matt rolled the TV cart closer to the fireplace. Catherine and Victoria placed the folding chairs in a semicircle around it. Once everything was in place, all they could do was wait.

"Matt, do you have a sec?" Catherine nodded her head toward the opposite side of the room.

Matt made eye contact with her and followed her to a corner away from everyone.

"I don't want to freak you out—and take this with a grain of salt. I mean, we're all under a lot of pressure right now and we've been through a lot." Catherine twisted a long, black curl. "But it's Darin."

"What about him?"

"I honestly wrestled with whether I should say this or not, but I've had a weird feeling all day. I just can't shake it." Catherine pressed her eyes together and released a sharp breath. "He was talking in his sleep last night."

"What do you mean?" Matt pinched his eyebrows together. "What was he saying?"

"He was, I dunno, apologizing. He kept saying he was so sorry and that he didn't mean to—didn't know it would happen."

"Is that all?" Matt asked.

"No." Catherine shook her head. "He kept saying something about Jim. And how Jim had tricked him. Or maybe Darin tricked Jim—Dr. Westbrook. It was . . . so weird."

"I knew it. I *knew* it!" Matt whispered. "Something felt off from the second he woke up with that bogus story about a bomb being strapped to him. I knew he was lying. What else is he hiding?"

"Matt"—Catherine placed her hands on his shoulders—"it may have just been a nightmare. Don't confront him on this, please."

"Why not? He might hold the answer to where we are. Where our families are. He's holding something back. I felt it in the beginning and you just confirmed it."

"Maybe." Catherine bit her lower lip. "Or maybe it was just a nightmare. I dunno, it *did* feel really intense. But if it's nothing, then you're going to divide the whole group with an accusation like that."

"Fine," Matt agreed. "I'll stay quiet, for now. But caution signs are up in my mind."

"Come on, let's go watch the tape."

"Hey, did the power kick on yet?" Matt called, walking toward the group. Catherine followed.

"Nope. Like, this is not going to work. No way," Kim said. "I can't believe you made my boyfriend go out into that heinous storm."

"Did you expect Cody to trudge through the snow by

himself?" Catherine asked. "Besides, he volunteered. So did Darin, Justin, and Nathan."

"Who said anything about Na-Na-Na-Nathan?" Kim laughed, then fluffed her feathered blond hair.

"So rude," Victoria muttered. "I think it's great. The more people who know how to run the generator, the better."

"Then why aren't you out there?" Stacy asked.

"I will, once the snow melts," Victoria said. "I've never ridden a bicycle before. Now isn't the time for me to learn."

"It's not a real bike anyway." Kim rolled her eyes.

"A stationary bike is still a bike," Matt said. "Victoria, I'll teach you. It's pretty easy, and you don't even have to balance."

The front door slammed open. Darin stood there, covered in snow. "Anything?" he asked.

Matt clicked on the TV. Nothing. "Nope."

"You got the gennie dug out?" Catherine asked.

"Mostly," Darin said. "The engine turned over, but they only pedaled for a few minutes. We'll take turns. I'll be back." He flipped the light switch to "on." "Let me know if the lights turn on, okay?"

"Sure thing, Lance-Darin," Stacy said.

Darin opened his mouth to say something but instead shook his head and turned to leave.

"Bye-bye." Stacy waved just the tips of her fingers.

"Ugh, this is, like, so dumb," Kim said. "How much longer is it going to be? And why aren't you out there helping, Matt? You're the only guy who didn't volunteer."

"He told you already!" Catherine yelled. "His wrist is still sore from when he slipped during the flood. He doesn't want to risk reinjuring it."

"When you killed Kyle?" Kim raised an eyebrow. "I mean, let him die?"

"Shut up, Kim! You don't know what you're talking about." Matt gritted his teeth. "If you're so bored, why don't you go shovel? Or better yet, go back to your cabin."

"You wait until I tell Rhett. He's going to kick your—"

The lights in the room flickered like a dying flame then went dark.

"I better tell Lance-Darin," Stacy said, breaking the silence and skipping to the door. She pulled it open and stepped out onto the wraparound porch. "Hey! Lance-Darin! The lights came on for a second."

"Way to let all the cold air in," Matt said. "The place just finally warmed up."

"Sorry." Stacy shrugged, shivered, and closed the door once she was back inside.

The lights flickered again, but this time stayed fully illuminated. Matt walked past Stacy and outside, careful to shut the door behind him. He made his way around the porch above the generator.

"Good job, guys," Matt said, peering over the edge at Justin, Cody, Rhett, and Darin. Darin sat atop the modified generator on the bike. He pedaled fast; his hot breath hung in the frigid air. "Lights are on."

"You guys go in." Darin huffed. "I'll be right behind you."

Matt watched Justin, Cody, and Rhett trudge through a narrow path they'd created in the deep snow. They used their shovels as walking sticks. The same shovels they would use to create a mass grave when the ground thawed.

Once inside, the boys removed their shoes and outerwear and replaced them with blankets and fresh socks.

"I ain't never been this cold," Cody said.

"Except when you were cryogenically frozen," Victoria said, smiling.

"That's true, little lady. Very true." Cody huddled in front of the fire.

Darin filed in a few minutes later. He dusted snow off his feathered brown hair.

"There should be enough stored power to keep it going for a few hours," Darin said. "You guys are going to need to find some oil or something for the gears—everything seems really tight."

"We'll see what we can find," Matt said. "I'm gonna start the next tape if anyone's interested."

"Not me," Kim said. "Rhett come here. I need to talk to you."

"I want to see the tape," Rhett said.

"Rhett!" Kim placed a hand on her hips and stomped a foot.

Rhett let out an exhausted sigh and lumbered over to Kim on the stage area.

"Good riddance," Matt said. He picked up a tape marked "7" and pushed it into the VCR. "What do you have to tell us today, Dr. Westbrook?"

The snow on the screen was replaced by jarring alarms and the scientist's red face. Gauze had been taped over his ears with white athletic tape. He held his head and muttered, "Dear listener, I regret to tell you, I've made the difficult decision of killing myself."

CHAPTER 3

"The alarms, they've been blaring for—well, it seems I've lost count. I've done everything to fix the underlying issue. It's the seventeen-year-olds. They're failing again. My attempts to fix the column have been unsuccessful." The man looked to the ceiling and released a desperate breath. "Sometimes, during the busiest parts of the day, I get used to the constant ringing of the alarm. Then all the feeding machines stop, the filtration systems rest, and the computers go to sleep, but I don't! I haven't slept since this started. Not one wink."

Dr. Westbrook began muttering incomprehensible sentences and paced. Soon, he was behind the camera and showed the seventeen-year-old column. Stacks of pods on shelves all blinked yellow. Warning. The sound was deafening. Matt pressed the fast-forward button while straining his neck to stare at the screen. In a flash, he saw the man's living quarters. An unmade bed and stacks of half-empty canned food littered the room. It looked like a hoarder's paradise. Finally, the camera settled onto the tripod, and Dr. Westbrook came back into frame.

"He looks terrible," Matt said.

"In the military, they use sleep deprivation as a form of torture. Did you know that? Of course you don't, why would you? I'm in a room with over five thousand people, and I've never felt more alone. Dear listener, do not feel guilty. I took this position on willingly. I thought I could be your savior." He removed his coke-bottle glasses and hung his head, revealing a small bald spot on the crown. "But the alarms are making me go mad. Please know, my intentions—from the very start—were good. Now, I must bid you adieu." He held his finger and thumb in the shape of a gun and pointed it at his temple before the tape went black.

"No!" Matt jumped up and smashed the fast-forward button in with his thumb.

Nothing but black.

"There's the crazy Westbrook I knew," Darin said.

"Stop it!" Matt said. "Look at all he went through to save us."

"Like he said, he volunteered." Darin stood, and his chair tipped over. "And he obviously didn't kill himself."

Matt squinted at him. Darin was right.

"Remember, he woke me up to help transport you guys? You saw him dead. Crushed, I think was your exact word."

"Then what happened?" Justin asked. "I hear you, man, but he looked pretty crazy."

"How would I know what happened?" Darin righted

his chair and sat. "He woke me up the same day he moved all of you."

"According to you," Matt said. His conversation with Catherine about Darin echoed in the back of his mind.

"Whatever," Darin said. "I'm not going over this with you again. I don't know anything."

"It's late," Catherine said. "Maybe clearer heads will prevail tomorrow."

She walked toward the rolled-up sleeping bags on the opposite side of the room. The varnish on the basketball court had peeled away years ago. Much of the wood had curled up and made it uneven. *A tripping hazard and lawsuit waiting to happen,* Kyle would have said. Catherine picked up a nylon bag and unrolled it in the center court, where kids from years past tipped off the start of a basketball game.

"I'm with Catherine," Stacy said. "Lance-Darin, wanna keep me warm?"

Justin furrowed his brow and crossed his arms in front of his chest.

"I think I'll sleep by the fire." Darin stared at Matt for a moment, then said to Stacy, "Alone."

"Your loss," Stacy said.

Matt wanted to interrogate Darin, but no one else seemed interested. They didn't know what Catherine had heard. Deep down, he was certain Darin was holding something back—maybe he knew the location of the cave. Instead, Matt lay next to Cody and Justin on the warped court.

"How about we get some mattresses from the cabins next time we go out, chief?" Justin asked.

"Do whatever you want." Matt rolled over and pressed his eyes shut.

"Chill out, man," Justin said.

"Sorry." Matt cringed. "Yeah, a mattress would be good right about now. Maybe after the snow melts."

"No worries, chief," Justin responded.

Matt found sleep quickly, but it was fitful. He was in his backyard standing on his AstroTurf lawn with a soggy tennis ball in his grip. Dutifully sitting, with his tail sweeping from side to side, was his beloved Saber. His eyes were fixed on the toy, pink tongue hanging from his mouth. Matt threw the ball but his dog didn't chase after it. Saber stared at him with familiar and comforting green eyes and led him into the house. "Wait!" Matt ran after him. "Come here, buddy." Before Matt opened the back door to let them both in, he knelt down and pet Saber. "I missed you."

He slid the sliding glass door sideways and walked in first. When he turned, Saber was gone and the kitchen phone was ringing. Matt ran across the faded linoleum and picked up the yellow receiver. "Hello?"

"Matt!"

"Mom?"

"Matty, where are you?"

"I'm—I'm home. You called me at home." Matt stretched the cord as far as it would go around the corner, searching the house.

"Matt, your father and I have specific instructions for you."

"Mom, I miss you and Dad so much! Please, you have to come home."

"We want that more than anything. But we can't come home until you finish your dinner."

"My what? What are you talking about? Mom, this is serious."

"Just make sure you eat all your food."

Click!

Matt held the phone up to his ear until he heard an operator come on and say, "If you'd like to make a call, please hang up," followed by aggressive beeping.

Matt replaced the receiver on the wall unit and turned around. "What the?" The empty kitchen table had been filled with cans. Bulging and swollen cans. He picked one up. The ripped label for green beans slipped from his fingers. Black sludge oozed from the top. He dropped it and stared at the massive pile of leaking tins. "No!" He opened a cabinet, and dozens of cans tumbled from the overly full space. He tugged on the dishwasher and gagged. Black muck sprayed out of the water line; he struggled to close it.

"This isn't happening. Mom! Dad!"

Matt ran into the living room and tripped. He landed in a wretched sea of foaming black residue amongst thousands of cans. He looked toward the ceiling and saw it had been replaced with a stories-high skyscraper of canned food. It swayed back and forth unsteadily. Matt tried to get to his feet but kept sliding and falling. Landing on his back, he heard the tower crumble, and all he could do was place his arms around his head.

"Matt." He felt a hand on his shoulder, but the voice sounded miles away. "Matt, wake up."

He blinked hard. "Catherine. Oh man."

"Nightmare?"

"Yeah," he said miserably.

"Me too," Catherine said. "Darin's not the only one, right?"

"Yeah," Matt said. "I guess."

"Forget about that right now." Catherine stood. "Come look outside."

Matt used the back of his hand to wipe the sleep from his eyes then jumped to his feet. His muscles were stiff. On one of the earlier tapes, he'd heard Dr. Westbrook wondering what fresh hell he was in store for that day. That statement resonated with Matt more than ever. He stared out the window into a sea of white. Nothing but snow. Deep snow. So much so that he wasn't sure where the snow stopped, and the buildings began.

"Come on, help us decide," Catherine said.

"Where is everyone?" Matt scanned the empty room.

"Outside," Catherine said. "You were sleeping really hard; I didn't want to wake you."

Matt wrapped a blanket around himself, slipped on his shoes, and stepped out onto the frigid porch. Snow was up to his mid-thigh.

"Whoa," Matt said.

"Whoa is right, partner," Cody said.

"Ma-Matt, can you see the sun?" Nathan asked.

"What?" Matt shook his head, still not fully awake. "That's why I'm out here?"

"Yes," Catherine laughed. "I know it's silly; call it cabin fever. But there's no sun."

"Yes, there is," Kim whined. "See that brighter spot, like, behind the clouds? This is so lame. I'm going in."

Matt squinted at the sky. "I mean, I'm sure there's a sun. But like Kim said, it's behind the clouds."

"Then why haven't we seen a sunset?" Cody asked.

"I know," Rhett said.

Everyone turned to the jock.

"You-you do?" Nathan asked.

"I grew up in a small mountain town in Washington. We were actually in a valley. Mountains surrounded us, so we never saw the, um"—he snapped his fingers—"what do you call it? The horizontal? So it just got slowly light then slowly dark out. Never saw the sun rise or set."

"There you have it, folks," Justin said, walking toward the door. "Mystery solved by my buddy Rhett. Waddya say we get some breakfast."

Matt turned to Cody. "That was weird."

"We was just stallin'." Cody led Matt back into the main cabin. "Everyone was waking up and bein' loud. You've seemed really tired lately, so Catherine and I devised this distraction. Only lasted a few minutes, but I swear, those extra five minutes on the snooze button are the best sleep I ever got."

"Oh geez, an alarm clock." Matt walked in and shook the snow from his tapered jeans. "Talk about a blast from the past."

"Chief, you want to watch another one of those tapes of yours?" Justin yelled.

"Sure," Matt said, but he had a sinking feeling in his stomach. The hollowness in your abdomen that formed when you knew you were about to get grounded or run into an ex.

"Br-breakfast?" Nathan handed Matt an MRE of powdered eggs. "Is this o-okay?"

"Thanks, Nathan," Matt said, "but I think we should probably keep these for when we leave camp, you know? They're lighter."

"Sorry," Nathan said.

"Don't apologize." Matt turned to the group. "Hey, everyone, grab yourself a can of whatever you want. Please don't eat the MREs. We'll save those for when we travel to find our parents, okay?

"Ravioli for breakfast?" Kim stuck out her tongue.

"Gag me with a spoon," Stacy echoed.

"Keep it up, and I just might," Catherine whispered, then handed Matt an open can of sliced pears. "Here."

"Thanks," he said. "Well, tape eight or bust. Wait, where's Darin?"

"Lance-Darin? He's clearing the snow and riding the generator bike," Stacy said. "He said he didn't want it to become fully buried again. Someone else might need to take a turn when he gets back, so it's fully charged."

"Sh-should we wait?" Nathan asked.

"Nah," Justin said. "He can watch—"

"I don't want to watch," Nathan said. "I'm going to switch with him."

"You okay?" Justin asked.

Nathan's shoulders slumped, and he walked out of the room. His tall frame seemed thinner today, more slight somehow.

The shuddering sound of gears popping and grinding interrupted Justin.

CHAPTER 4

Matt looked to Catherine and Cody. They stared back, wide-eyed. Then they ran to the window and waited.

After a few minutes of nothing, Matt turned to the group. "Let's get the tapes watched while we can." Matt powered the TV and VCR on and slid tape eight in.

The scientist appeared, smiling—almost jovial. Alarms sounded, but he seemed unbothered. His wiry hair had long since lost its color and was fully gray. His face was plump, and he looked healthy.

"Look at that deranged man," Darin said.

"How's the gennie?" Matt asked, ignoring Darin's insult. *This man saved our lives, there's nothing deranged about this.*

"Not too bad." He had a blanket wrapped around him. Snow dripped from his feathered light brown hair. He pointed at the TV with his narrow chin. "His eyes—look, they're crazy."

"He seems happy." Matt deflected Darin's comment.

"Good morrow, gentle listener! Today is my birthday—I've lost a few days here and there, but I'm confident today is the day. I am seventy years old. I've celebrated the last forty birthdays here. Isn't that remarkable?" Dr. Westbrook smiled like the Cheshire cat. "The first decade or so were quite fine. The loneliness didn't get to me until sometime in my forties; that's when I started documenting my days. Youth is something to be desired. You're resilient and can handle anything. If only my dear Darin had been as spirited as promised."

Everyone turned to Darin. He rolled his eyes and shrugged in response. The front door opened, taking the attention off him. A blast of freshly chilled air swept into the room. Nathan's clothes and head were caked in snow.

"The generator is as charged as it's going to be," Nathan said, then walked to the fireplace. "It's really coming down hard out there. I couldn't pedal anymore; the gears are frozen."

"But I digress," Dr. Westbrook continued on the screen. "Weary traveler, you have been with me for three decades in a matter of minutes through my recordings. And you have been my motivation to remain. The alarms have been constant for some time now, but I've grown used to them. Come, see what travesty has transpired."

He turned the camera toward an empty column. Then panned to an area with pods piled carelessly on the ground. Next to them were black body bags stacked neatly on top of each other.

"You see, the fifteen-year-olds didn't make it. Not a single one. We lost all one-hundred and six of them."

"Stop the tape," Rhett said.

Nathan jumped up and paused it.

Rhett sat hunched over in his chair. His shoulders heaved, but he made no sound.

"Rhett, it's okay. Like, tell me what's wrong so I can help you," Kim said.

Tears streamed down Rhett's face. "My sister, she was fifteen. She was in one of those body bags, like trash!" He cradled his face in his hands. "She was so smart, not like me. When I was failing math, no one could get through to me like her. She is—was—so patient and nice. Never made me feel stupid. Secretly, she was my best friend. I can't believe the last time I hugged her before cryosleep was—was the last time ever!"

"Oh, Rhett, babe, I'm so sorry." Kim rubbed his muscular back.

"Rhett . . ." Matt tried to find the words, but nothing came.

Kim led him off toward the opposite side of the room, where they'd slept the previous night. He lay on a sleeping bag over Kim's lap, and she stroked his hair while he cried. For once, she didn't make a situation about her.

"We need to know what happened to everybody else. I need to see what happened to my family. Can we just watch the stupid tape?" Stacy said.

Nathan clicked it back on. The scientist continued.

"My dear seventeen-year-olds were the problematic ones. The reason for the initial breach. Troublesome as they were, I ultimately got them stabilized. But it must have triggered something, because as soon as they were fixed, the fifteen-year-old column quit. Died immediately. There was no saving them. But I won't let that happen again."

Matt's chest tightened. He looked around the room and saw eyes wide, mouths frozen open in horror, and others shifting in their seat toward the person next to them. It was as if they were watching a slasher film, and not real life.

The camera shook, and a loud bang followed. Overhead lights flickered behind Dr. Westbrook.

"Ah yes, the apocalypse is still in its full fury. There is no stopping it! I will be moving my unstable columns to a site called HZRD. The first ones to move will be my hardy seventeen-year-olds. I'll take ten at a time, or at least that's the goal. Once they're all successfully relocated, I will move the rest of the pods. Over five thousand in total. 'Tis a massive undertaking, but I am up for the challenge."

"Wait." Catherine stood and paused the tape. "Why move the stable ones? That doesn't make any sense."

"Because he's crazy. Like Jack Torrance in *The Shining* crazy," Darin said.

"Or maybe he needs to have everyone in one spot to take care of them," Matt said. "Play it up."

"But where's HZRD? Is this HZRD?" Catherine pressed.

"Hell if I know," Darin replied.

"Hang on. Before, when he was talking about Rhett's sister, he said 'we,' Darin," Matt said. "Were you there?"

"What? No." Darin's face contorted as if he'd eaten something rancid. "He also called you weary traveler. No one has traveled in over forty years according to him. He's nuts. He probably uses we, I, and us interchangeably, depending on what personality he's using that day."

"It just seemed like maybe someone was there. He said 'we,' not 'I,'" Matt said.

"Like I said, he was crazy," Darin replied. He sat with his legs splayed out, slouched so far down in his seat, it looked like he might slip off his chair. "I wasn't awake. Period. End of story."

"Let's get this over with." Stacy started the tape. "And no more interruptions. We need to know what happens to everyone else. And for the record, *I* believe you, Lance-Darin."

"Unfortunately, the test site, HZRD, doesn't have the freezing capabilities, and I will be forced to wake you all. But I will take care of you. Become your leader. It is time to get to work. Goodbye for now. And as you'll soon see, my intentions are good."

"There were ten of us, including the girl who died," Matt said. "That means there are others in our column waiting to be moved."

"Or he already mo-mo-moved them, and we were the last," Nathan said. "The other seventeen-year-olds cou-could be at HZRD."

"Maybe this place is HZRD," Catherine said.

"Then he would have known about the power and VCR, right?" Victoria asked. "I don't know, this seems . . . calculated to me."

Darin stared intently at the floor, avoiding all eye contact.

"Did you guys notice the way he looked?" Cody asked. "I know Darin and I were the only ones to see him alive after our initial freezing, but don't you think he looked the same age?"

"Yeah, he did," Darin said. "This was filmed shortly before he woke me and moved you guys."

"Wait, you were there," Matt said. "Were we the first or the last?"

"First." Darin looked down. "He was shutting things down when he unhooked you. I don't think the others in your column are still alive."

CHAPTER 5

"So that's it?" Catherine gasped. "We're the only seven-teen-year-olds left?"

Darin stared forward and nodded.

"No way!" Stacy yelled. "No way they're all dead!"

"What about the other age columns?" Matt stood.

"As far as I know, and from what I could see," Darin swallowed, "they were all still alive."

"Yeah, but that was days ago," Justin said.

"And what about HZRD?" Cody asked, pressing his palms into his eyes.

"I-I can't believe so many people have perished." Nathan wrapped his arms around himself. "Wh-why did we get to live?"

"Let's see what the last tape says." Matt nodded in Victoria's direction.

"I need to know what happened to my parents!" Victoria pressed in the final tape. "Shh."

"Hello, gentle listener, greetings to you all. I've been very busy these last six months. First, I must start with the grim news. I spent much of the time prepping and burning the corpses from the fifteen-year-old column. It was a task that had to be done. My dear seventeen-year-olds have held strong. I will move them first. Come see." He panned over to a pod with "#20" on it. Matt recognized it immediately and rubbed the area above his heart where his old uniform had the same number embroidered on it. "Here are eight recordings of our time together. I'll place this final one in once I'm done. Number twenty, whoever you are, you will have our history for when we start this new life together."

Dr. Westbrook used a key around his utility belt to unlock the cryopod. Matt lay inside in suspended animation. Staring at himself, so still and helpless, sent shivers down Matt's spine. The doctor carefully placed the tapes around his body, like lining a coffin with flowers.

Everyone turned to Matt. "Now we know how I got the tapes," he said.

"Guess you weren't lying, chief," Justin said. "It really was random."

The scientist continued. "You'll be transported in this fine piece of equipment. I had to add a few modifications, like the solar panels, but it seems to be up and running just fine."

The lens zoomed in on the same Army-issued truck they'd first seen when they escaped their pods just days ago. The same truck they'd found Darin passed out in. The same truck Matt had stood on and lost his grip on Kyle. Matt rubbed his wrist; it was nothing more than a dull ache now. But Kyle was still gone, and Matt carried that weight.

The camera rested on what Matt guessed was the tripod, and Dr. Westbrook stood—something he rarely did in his videos. He wore a white jacket over his shirt with a yellow bandana hanging from his neck. Long, tan cargo pants housed a utility belt of treasures. Matt recognized the Swatch around the doctor's wrist from when he was crushed. A boxy yellow rectangle, the size of a loaf of bread, hung awkwardly off the belt. A Geiger counter. Matt had only seen them on the news after the Chernobyl meltdown. On the face of the Geiger counter was a round circle with a needle-style gauge.

"My calculations were correct," Dr. Westbrook said, beaming. "I can fit exactly ten pods onto the bed of the truck. I will take you all to the HZRD site and will give you further instructions or record another tape for you to review while we move the remaining pods. Oh, this is an exciting day indeed. It's your first day of your new life. Cryosurvival is no longer sustainable. I will move each and every one of you myself—all five thousand of you— minus the fifteen-year-old column, of course. Now we must survive together. Gentle listener, you will soon see how well-intended I am. I can't wait for you to meet me."

He removed the camera from the tripod and captured a quick shot of the truck before ending the recording.

"What the?" Matt sprang from his seat and to the VCR. "Was that?"

Matt rewound and hit play, then pause. He pressed the pause button repeatedly, moving it frame by frame, wrenching his neck to see the shot.

"See?!" Matt said.

Darin was paused on the screen near the back of

the truck, mid-jump, holding a length of rope. Around his waist was the brown Everlast weightlifting belt that Darin had claimed was a bomb.

"And?" Darin said. "Yeah, that's me. I told you I was there. I was securing a pod."

"Right, sorry," Matt said. "I think I'm just grasping at straws. I just really want you to have the answers, or at least more information."

"Yeah, well . . ." Darin paused. "I don't know anything that would be helpful."

Matt stared at him but said nothing.

"Okay," Stacy said. "If anything, this video proves he was there just like he already said."

"I honestly don't care if you guys believe me or not. I know what happened, and I've told you everything. Believe it or not. That's not on me," Darin said.

"So that's it?" Victoria asked. "That was the last video?"

"Looks like it," Cody said. "Never had a chance to film the instructions for us."

"Now what?" Victoria asked. "We're snowed in. What can we do?"

"We need to find the cave," Matt said.

"I agree." Darin sat forward. "But where do we even start searching? The air was terrible when I left there, the weather was deadly, and worst of all, we're not going anywhere for days, maybe weeks. The snow is so deep."

"Well," Stacy said, standing, "while you guys figure that out, I think the rest of us should go sledding."

"I've never been sledding," Victoria said.

"Really?" Justin asked. "There's a lot you haven't done."

"And plenty I have!" Victoria nervously twisted her long braid. "I've been to five continents, eaten at countless Michelin star restaurants, learned Spanish and Portuguese, flown in private jets, met Reagan and . . ." She broke down in tears. "None of that matters. I can't do basic things. I can't do survival things. I only know my Manhattan life. Look at all of you. You all have skills. What am I good for?"

"Oh, Victoria," Stacy said. "I'm just as useless as you. And it turns out we have a lot more in common than I thought."

"Do-don't feel b-bad." Nathan hugged Victoria. His tall, lanky frame encompassed her petite body. "Stop crying. These gu-guys will help. Cody taught me how to use the ge-generator. And Matt sho-showed me the flint."

"Victoria, we'll teach you anything you want," Matt said. "Come on. Let's go out to the deck for a few minutes. Get some fresh air, and I'll explain the basics of the flint and steel wool. We can practice on the existing fire inside after, okay?"

She dried her eyes on Nathan's shirt and nodded at Matt with red-rimmed eyes. "I'd like that."

"Hey, listen up." Matt clapped his hands. "Anyone who doesn't know how to make fire, grab a coat or blanket and meet me on the deck."

"No *thanks*," Kim yelled. "I've got my beefcake, and he'll take care of me."

"Kim!" Stacy yelled. "Come on, if I have to do this, so do you."

"No way." Kim's eyes grew wide, and she tilted her head toward Rhett, whose head was still in her lap. "Like, I'm not leaving him in his time of need."

"It's fine," Matt said. "I'll show you later. Or Rhett can if he knows how."

Matt tossed a blanket over his shoulders and waited at the door for Stacy and Victoria.

"I'm coming too," Catherine asked. "I think I could figure it out in a pinch, but I'd like a lesson."

"Of course," Matt said. "Maybe we should have everyone get a refresher so Rhett and Kim can be alone. He seems really heartbroken about his sister."

"I'll tell everyone," Catherine said.

Somewhere in the distance, gears popped and grinded. The floor under Matt's feet trembled. He pressed his ear to the door but only heard the wind. Soon, everyone but Rhett and Kim joined him at the entryway.

"Ready?" Matt asked.

"Yep," Justin said. "Even though this is a waste of my time, chief."

Matt stepped outside, and his breath was immediately stolen by the glacial air. Snow fell so quickly, it seemed unreal. Like a movie set.

"Whoa!" Justin pushed his way to the railing on the deck. "Check out this drift. It's hardcore."

"No way," Matt said. "It's as high as the deck railing. This isn't good."

"Why?" Stacy asked. "We can totally sled off the side of the deck once it's nicer out. Victoria can finally have her first experience."

"Seriously?" Matt held the bridge between his eyes.

"It means we're going to be stuck here for a very long time."

"Sorry," Darin said. "I know you guys wanted to get out of here ASAP."

"What's with this 'you guys,' mantra, man?" Justin asked. "You never refer to yourself as part of the group."

"I—I dunno," Darin said. "It's just—wait. Nathan, are you okay? What are you doing?"

Nathan stood frozen, his trembling arm pointed straight out. Matt peered in the direction he indicated. Snow cascaded down the mountain face in what looked like a large, pluming cloud and enveloped the trees. A small cabin on the outskirts was swallowed within an instant, nothing more than an appetizer for the incoming avalanche.

"Get inside!" Matt yelled. "Hurry!"

CHAPTER 6

"Nathan, get inside!" Matt desperately pulled on Nathan's shoulder, trying to wake him from his trance.

Nathan stared back at him with blank eyes.

"Please!" Matt pleaded. "Help!"

"We got you," Justin said. Darin followed behind him.

"Come on," Darin said. "Snap out of it."

Darin bear-hugged Nathan, locked his arms behind him, and pushed forward. Nathan's hips swung back toward Darin. Next, Darin stepped his right leg out and behind Nathan's long legs. Nathan fell onto Darin's thigh and instinctively reached out for him.

"What are you doing?" Matt asked. "Don't hurt him."

"He's okay. Westbrook taught me that move," Darin said. "Drag him in!"

Justin, being the strongest, slipped his arms under Nathan's armpits and pulled. Matt held a foot and Darin the other. It was only a few feet away, but Nathan was dead weight and Matt's forearms burned.

Catherine stood at the door, ready to slam it shut behind them.

"Get something to block the door," Matt yelled, looking frantically around the gym. The open space didn't have much to block the entrance.

"On it." Rhett and Kim had rejoined the group by the entrance. He rolled the TV cart toward the door. "Get some chairs."

"Here." Victoria handed him a folding chair.

Rhett wedged it under the door handle, then tipped the TV cart on its side and shoved it next to the door. The TV smashed against the hardwood floor, shattering the screen.

"Now what? What do we do?" Stacy asked, her face stricken with panic.

"I don't know. Find a tub? Like you do for a tornado?" Catherine suggested.

"No," Matt said. "The stage—no windows, it's our best bet. Run!"

The low rumble became a freight train in his short sprint to the stage. The entire ground below him shook. His ears rang, the room spun, and Matt fell onto his hands mere feet from the stage. He crab-walked backward, looking at the window. A wave of snow smashed against it and swallowed the cabin. Snow caked the windows. He felt hands pulling him onto the stage and faintly heard someone yelling for Nathan.

Nathan had come to his senses at some point and was running across the gym. His thin arms thrust forward like windmills, his gait was overly large, and his eyes were so unnaturally wide, Matt thought he looked like a caricature of himself. The roof creaked under the weight of the snow.

The tall, lanky boy from Utah stopped dead in his tracks and look up at the support beam that ran along the center of the A-frame cabin. It splintered in the middle of the roof, and one half came careening down like a cricket bat—Nathan was the ball. He ducked, then sprinted toward the stage.

Nathan hadn't planned on the centripetal force.

"Duck!" Matt screamed.

Smack!

The log connected with the back of Nathan's legs and butt, throwing him forward. He landed with a sick thud.

Matt jumped down to help him, then he heard the other half of the log break free from the center. It came swinging down toward the stage. Matt dove to the left of the theater area. The log bounced against the stage, denting it.

"Nathan!" Victoria called.

"I'm okay." Nathan slowly stood. "I'm just a little worse for the wear."

Matt heard another sick creaking noise and watched in horror as the left side of the aluminum roof collapsed, bringing mounds of snow down onto his friend.

But it didn't just cave in. It folded inward as if it was connected to a hinge on the long side of the cabin. The metal bang was deafening as it connected with the wall. Snow plumed, creating a hazy white cloud. Before it completely settled, the opposing wall fell in a similar fashion.

"Nathan!" Victoria called out.

Matt jumped down next to her and grabbed her. "No! It's not safe."

"We can't leave him!" Victoria said.

"Avalanche!" Catherine screamed.

Matt gripped a handful of Victoria's long dress and heaved her up onto the stage, then scrambled up after.

"Get back!" Matt yelled.

Before he could react, the front wall of the cabin toppled onto the rubble. He found himself as far back on the stage as he could go.

"We're going to die!" Stacy cried.

A wave of snow pinned Matt to the cinderblock wall so hard, he thought he might actually break through it. Frigid snow filled his ears and nose holes like quicksand. As soon as he felt the momentum shift, he pressed his hands against the wall and pushed himself backward. He fell and found himself staring at a drift against the wall.

He frantically reached into the drift for his friends. Justin and Rhett had gotten themselves out on their own.

"Help!" Matt yelled at them.

He'd been in this same situation before. Only last time it was pods, and Catherine and Cody were out. He punched his hand into the drift and felt for anything. A hand gripped his forearm. Matt pulled back as hard as he could without falling. Frizzy, red hair popped out of the snow. Stacy gasped for air, then immediately melted into a puddle of tears.

Matt turned to his left and saw that Cody and Darin had been pulled to safety. As soon as they caught their breath, they became part of the search team.

"Catherine! Victoria!" Matt yelled.

He reached into the snow again, but this time came up empty-handed. With each punch, the skin on his knuckles tore little by little, leaving pink streaks behind.

A hand and wrist reached up from the snow.

"I'm coming!" He ran to the hand and pulled.

Justin reached over the side of Matt and joined in. Finally, the face appeared.

Catherine.

She rolled onto her side and coughed.

"We've got Kim and Victoria," Rhett announced.

"Is that everyone?" Matt asked.

"No." Victoria sat up, and brought her knees up to her chest. "We're missing Nathan."

Matt sucked in a cold, dry breath. The silence was deafening. He slowly walked to the edge of the stage, trying to process the scene. He felt his chest tighten and tried to focus and calm his breath. The temperature had dropped at least fifty degrees, and every breath felt like tiny, sharp icicles were gathering in Matt's lungs.

The last he'd seen, the green metal roof had split down the middle. Each side came to rest against the long wall on its respective side. Now, after the second avalanche, he saw the true destruction. It had completely downed the front wall. For a brief moment, Matt was thankful it hadn't been pushed into the theater area where it would have crushed them. It, like the roof, hadn't broken or splintered. The avalanche simply tipped it forward into the room.

All support for the cabin was gone. It appeared the east wall had caved in first. It lay at an angle on top of the front wall. The west wall had fallen last. The mounds of snow were the icing on top. Only the cinderblock wall, backstage, remained. And it was likely to cave at any moment.

"Nathan." Matt jumped down onto the snow pile of rubble.

There was no excitement behind his voice. He knew. This wasn't a rescue mission.

It was a recovery.

Cody was the next one down, followed by Justin, then the rest.

Matt tried to push on the wall, but it was useless. Not even with all their might combined could they move the snow-covered walls and roof.

Matt crawled under a beam and reached around blindly. He held onto it and pulled as he shimmied out. Freezing snow slid up his shirt. He felt a thick cord. He pulled on the cable, but it wouldn't budge.

"What is this?" Matt said to no one. "What is this connected to?"

He clambered to the top of the pile toward another black cable poking out of the snow. The source was an eyelet screw that connected it to a log on one of the walls. Matt's face twisted in confusion.

"I found him!" Victoria yelled. "He's right here. Hurry! Help me!"

Matt dropped the cable and carefully walked to the spot from where he heard her voice. Rhett's legs poked out from the rubble next to Victoria's.

"Victoria, let go," Rhett said. "You're making this harder."

Victoria emerged first, her black dress caked with snow.

Rhett shimmied and stopped inch by inch until he was out. Two feet peeked from the rubble. The same way Matt had identified Kyle. He sucked in a sharp breath.

"Is he going to be okay?" Victoria asked. "He is, right?"

"Victoria . . ." Catherine pulled her into a hug.

With one hard yank, Rhett pulled Nathan free from the rubble.

A dusty white haze filled the cabin. They all huddled together around their dead friend's body.

CHAPTER 7

Before Matt could even gather his thoughts, the clouds parted and the sun shone brightly through the rubble. As if someone had flipped a switch. Intense heat coupled with swiftly melting snow created an unnatural and intense humidity.

Snow melted at an incredible speed. The scene reminded Matt of watching a National Geographic movie about Yellowstone in biology class. It had been a time-lapse video of winter melting away and spring beginning and turning into summer. The snow had evaporated, and a small green bud popped through the earth. In a matter of seconds, it had grown into a tulip, then died and wilted in the summer heat.

"What in the French toast is happening here?" Cody asked.

"This is insane!" Stacy said.

"Whoa," Matt said. "What the French is right."

What lay before Matt made him question his own sanity. Dozens of thin black cables hung loose from a pulley apparatus above them. All that remained of the cabin was the cinderblock and rebar-reinforced stage area. The rest of the cabin lay folded in on itself.

"What the hell?" Justin cupped his right hand over his forehead, shielding it from the bright light. "This is straight out of a sci-fi movie. Is some alien playing cat's cradle, and these pullies are the yarn?"

The cabin destruction left from the avalanches was showcased under powerful light and the blue skies above. Water flowed into cracks, melting snow as quickly as it came. All the water pooled toward the spot where the fireplace had been.

"We need to get out of here now," Matt said. "This place is unstable."

"Follow me," Cody said.

"What about Nathan?" Victoria cried.

"I'll get him," Rhett said. He nodded at Justin.

Justin held Nathan's limp wrists, and Rhett lifted Nathan's ankles.

Matt leapt over a cable, then ducked under another. He tripped and bashed his knees on what used to be the roof. He ducked and rolled, avoiding cables.

"You guys, watch out for the cables." Matt looked over his shoulder at Justin and Rhett. "They're every-where."

Then he saw it.

Nathan's face. He'd been avoiding it since they pulled him from the wreckage.

Blood oozed from his nose, mouth, and eyes. His crushed, sagging body looked like a wooden marionette doll that bounced and jiggled with each step Justin and Rhett took.

Matt turned away and swallowed bile that had gathered in this throat. *I shouldn't have left him behind. But what could I do?*

Matt followed Catherine on the partially intact wraparound porch to the backside of the cabin—technically the theater area. From the outside, the cinderblocks had been covered in logwood siding, concealing the industrial look. A support beam had fallen on the porch, and the deck angled sharply toward the ground.

"Victoria, you're the lightest. You go first." Darin pointed to the steep ramp. "We need to see if it'll hold."

"Excuse me?" Kim said. "I'm the thinnest. I'm a flyer for my squad, thank you very much."

"Fine!" Darin yelled. "Then you go!"

"Screw you. I'm not your guinea pig."

"Kim, if you don't shut your mouth—" Catherine started.

"No!" Victoria yelled. "Stop it! I can't take it!"

Victoria ran down the wobbly deck, screaming the entire time. It shifted from side to side with her erratic gait but held. She got to the edge and lowered herself down three feet until she was firmly on the ground.

"This is all our fault!" Victoria yelled. "All this fighting and finger pointing. Nathan is dead because we couldn't come together. This is *all* our fault!"

Matt swallowed hard and locked eyes with Catherine. She was next down the ramp, and once at the bottom, she embraced Victoria and stroked her hair.

One by one, they made their way down onto the

ground, where muddy water squelched up over their shoes and surrounded their ankles. The heat intensified, and Matt guessed it was over ninety degrees. His skin was slick with sweat and the air felt thick. Finally, Rhett and Justin gingerly carried Nathan's body over. Matt's palms sweat as he watched what was left of the porch bow and creak with each step.

"Where should we put him?" Justin asked, bowing his head.

"I don't know," Matt said. "Somewhere safe until we can bury him."

They all looked around, their faces mirroring what Matt was thinking. Was any place safe?

CHAPTER 8

"None of this makes any sense." Stacy collapsed onto the wet ground. "This has to be a bad dream."

"Poor Nathan." Matt ignored her, and instead walked around to the front of where the cabin had been. It wasn't like he had the answers.

Everyone but Stacy followed.

"He didn't have a chance," Darin said. "There was no way he could have survived the collapse like that. And I fear it's going to keep happening."

"What do you mean by that?" Matt asked.

"I mean, the apocalypse is obviously still ongoing. We're encountering more crappy weather." Darin held the bridge of his nose. "Look, fifteen minutes ago, it was a full-on blizzard. Now, it's ninety degrees, and most of the snow has melted. And why isn't it flooding? Where is all this water going?"

"This is just like the flood." Matt shook his head. "It's like it drained or something. I don't know!"

"Look at that!" Cody pointed to the side of the mountain filled with downed trees.

A few drifts that still remained looked like someone spilled chocolate-infused piña coladas, but most of the snow had melted, creating a sloppy mess. The avalanche chutes were clear. The largest scar carved through the forest, remnants of the avalanche that killed Nathan. Matt hung his head.

First Kyle. Now Nathan.

They hadn't even had a chance to give Kyle a proper burial before this mess unfolded. Now they had another body to add to that count.

"Matt," Catherine whispered into his ear. "I'm scared. What is this?"

He stared back toward the mountain. The scent of moist dirt and pine filled the air. Loud creaking echoed in the otherwise silent valley. One by one, trees sprung back up like someone had turned the page in a pop-up book. Needles cascaded to the ground from the swaying trees as the forest around righted itself to normal. Matt shook his head, trying to make sense of it all.

"I—I don't get it! I wish you could just get us out of here and back to the cave, Darin!" he screamed.

"Back off, kid." Darin stood almost a full head taller than Matt and was nearly as muscular as Justin. "I've been patient with you guys and your unrelenting questions—*accusations*, really. I know you think I have some sort of information that's going to explain this all away, but I don't. I'm just as puzzled as you."

"Then what is this place?" Kim's voice trembled.

"Like, what is happening? Holy crap, half of the cabins are, like, wiped out!"

"We know we're at HZRD, according to Westbrook. But who knows what HZRD is?" Darin said. "Westbrook royally screwed us when he brought us and left us in a forest."

"I thought you loved this place. Said the air was good and whatnot." Matt crossed his arms.

"The air *is* good. But this place is a natural disaster zone. He just should have kept us frozen," Darin said.

"And let us die?" Cody asked.

"Looks like that's gonna happen one way or the other here." Darin walked back toward the backside of the cabin, where Stacy had remained.

Matt looked to his friends. Kim had buried her face in Rhett's firm chest, and he hugged her, but his face was blank, expressionless. Justin stood tall, overlooking the camp. Cody rubbed the back of his neck.

Catherine turned to Matt, hugged him, and whispered, "I'm sorry. I'm going around back. I need to say goodbye to Nathan."

Rhett and Kim followed her.

Justin ran a hand through his sandy-blond hair and said, "Darin's right. We're screwed."

The adrenaline had worn off, and Matt was overcome with emotion. He felt his chest tighten, and tears spilled from his eyes. He crouched against the wall, brought his knees up to his chest, and wept like he hadn't done since he was a little kid.

"Hey, I didn't mean it, chief," Justin said. "It's probably not that bad."

"It's not you," Matt said in between sobs, "it's everything. None of this makes any sense. You saw it with your own eyes. The cabin, the trees, the avalanches, and the quick shifts in the weather. Now Nathan. Nathan, who wouldn't hurt a fly, was crushed to death. Pinned. He was so scared. I'll never get his desperate cries out of my head. I should've saved him."

"You saved the rest of us," Cody said. "You were right to have us wait. We're lucky we all weren't crushed. What happened to Nathan is a tragedy, but it's not your fault."

"Look how many have died. Dr. Westbrook, girl number seven whose name we don't even know, Kyle, and now Nathan. Darin's right. We're all doomed."

"Look, chief, you gotta pull it together," Justin said. "Everyone looks to you for answers—"

"Darin too," Cody interrupted.

"Yeah," Justin shifted, "*Lance-Darin* too. If you crack, everyone is going to lose it."

Matt pressed his palms into his eyes and stood. A wet spot from the melting snow stained the seat of his pants. Justin was right. Matt had to figure out something—even if it just meant getting them somewhere safer and leaving Camp New Beginnings.

"Should we go around back? Pay our respects to Nathan?" Cody asked.

"You go," Matt said. "I need to take a walk. I'm not ready to see him like that again."

Matt trudged through the mud. Behind him, the once large main cabin was now smashed flat. With the force of the avalanche, many of the cabins in Camp New Beginnings didn't have a chance. Something odd pulled at the back of his brain. Most of the collapsed cabins weren't piles of splintered sticks, but instead, they seemed to have just folded in on each other.

But that wasn't what drove him forward. The trees had sprung up like nothing had happened, and no one said a word. Maybe he was the only one who'd seen it happen. Or maybe they were too traumatized. Matt walked to the first trees near the edge of the camp. An old conifer that was once laid out by an intense avalanche now stood tall and erect. He couldn't make sense of it. What apocalyptic phenomenon had the force to flatten a tree, then revive it back to life?

CHAPTER 9

Once at the tree, Matt dropped to his knees. Pawing at the earth, he was positive he'd find something, *anything* to explain what he'd witnessed. Either that or he was going insane and imagining all of this. He paused for a moment and considered that. *Is this real? Are my friends real? Am I even here? Is this a dream in the cryosleep?*

A dull ache thumped in his left wrist. He rubbed the spot. *No, not a dream. I don't think you feel pain in dreams or hallucinations.* He dug like a frantic dog looking for a bone. The soft earth caked his hands with rich soil. Pine needles poked at his palms and fingertips, but he put it out of his mind and continued to dig.

"Where is it? What lifted you back up? Huh? Tell me!" he yelled. "Who did this? Is there someone underneath? Who are you? How'd you do it? Is this real? Of course it is. Nathan is dead. Kyle is dead. That's real!" Matt screamed until his throat was raw. He pounded the dirt.

A gentle hand touched his shoulder. Matt snapped back to himself.

"Matt, you gotta calm down," Cody said evenly. "You saw what happened to Nathan when he lost it."

"I did!" Matt stood. "And now we have to bury him. And Kyle. And Dr. Westbrook and some random, nameless girl—if we can even find them."

"Whoa, chief," Justin said. "Come back to reality with me for a minute, 'kay?"

Matt blinked hard, trying to calm his breath, wishing they hadn't seen him like this.

"I can't explain what's happening either," Justin said. "But let's just take a step back."

"A step back?" Matt scoffed. "I'd like to take a leap back. Back to when things were normal."

"None of this has made sense from the beginnin'," Cody said. "We were dropped off outside a camp that just so happened to have some food, water, a generator, and a dang VCR."

"Exactly!" Matt desperately splayed his muddy hands out in Cody's direction. "That's what I've been saying!"

"But maybe it's not meant for us to know," Cody said. "Like God. I don't understand why He decided it was time for an apocalypse, but it's not for me to understand. I just kept on livin' and trustin' He'd take care of me."

"All right, let's not drag religion into this," Justin said. "We all know that's garbage."

"Is not," Cody said.

"Yeah, I bet the other bazillion people who died didn't feel taken care of by your God," Justin replied.

"I hope you find Jesus Christ in your heart before it's your time," Cody said. "I'm more than happy to help get you there."

"Whatever." Justin rolled his eyes. "But the cowboy makes a good point. We're here, and things don't make sense, but neither did the apocalypse. Maybe this *is* the new normal. I'm not sure. But not everything has an answer, you know? Like women. Geesh, good luck ever trying to figure any of them out."

"Yeah," Matt said.

Justin smiled. Matt bet his smile got him out of a lot of trouble *before*. "And I know my parents sucked, but I don't want them to die. I want to save them. And everyone else. This place isn't all we thought it was cracked up to be."

"I know," Matt said. "We have to find everyone else. Wherever *that* is."

"Let's try and keep you out of the looney bin," Justin said. "While this pains me to admit, you've had the best plans so far." He cleared his throat. "You figure anything out with that tree?"

"No, the ground is still frozen under the surface. I need a shovel. Couldn't get past the topsoil." Matt wiped his hands on the logo of his *Commodore 64* shirt. "I need a shovel to see what's really down there."

"Speaking of that—" Cody said.

"I know," Matt said. "Come on, let's get this over with."

They walked in silence, which Matt was thankful for. He was still trying to make sense of everything and get his mind right. During the walk back, he closed his eyes and thought about his parents. When he entered high school, he started having "little episodes," as his mom called them. He'd get so overwhelmed that his chest felt tight, and he couldn't catch his breath. His mom taught him to fix his attention on something still, like the tile floor, and focus on breathing. She said it was sort of like meditation, and deemed it "Matt-itation." It became his saving grace, and he couldn't believe he'd forgotten about it until now. The moment he felt the tightening in his chest, he'd do his Matt-itation. He smiled at the memory.

The humidity from the melted snow combined with the intense heat made the air thick. Matt stared at the rubble and thought back to the first time he saw the cabin. He was so full of hope. Now he was filled with dread.

"Where'd you go?" Catherine met him where they'd had the firepit the night before.

"I needed a minute," Matt said. "How is everyone?"

"Kim seems a little shaken, but no worse for the wear. Rhett is really upset, almost withdrawn. I can't imagine seeing your sister tossed away in a heap of garbage bags." She nodded her head toward the two, who were holding each other on the ground. "Stacy is sad, Darin is withdrawn, and Victoria is traumatized. She hasn't left Nathan's body and keeps talking to him. I don't get it. They weren't close."

"She's sensitive. Plus, this is the first time she's probably ever witnessed death. Honestly, probably the first time anyone has, except you and Cody."

"And you," Catherine said.

"Right," Matt replied.

He followed Catherine to the back of the building until

he reached Nathan. All color had drained from him. Victoria stroked his brown hair and quietly sang a song Matt didn't recognize. He knelt by her and Nathan's body.

"What are you thinking, Victoria?" Matt asked.

"Life's precious." Her gaze remained fixed on Nathan's face.

"It is," Matt said. "Do you think it would be okay if we moved him away from the cabin?"

"Why?" Victoria finally looked at Matt. "He seems peaceful here."

"He's gone, you know that, right?"

"Yes." She covered her face and cried quietly into her hands. "I suppose he needs a proper burial like the others."

"Absolutely. As soon as the ground is fully thawed—and that'll be really soon—we'll have a funeral. Until then, maybe take a break. Didn't you promise to braid Catherine's hair since she did yours?"

Victoria touched the long plait that ran down her back.

"Come on." Catherine pulled Victoria to her feet. "Good luck braiding this curly mess."

The girls walked hand-in-hand, and it brought brief comfort to Matt.

Then he remembered the grisly task that awaited him.

"Rhett, Justin, can I get your help?" Matt called.

Darin followed the two over. Matt gritted his teeth.

"We need to get him out of here. Let's put him under a tarp until we can dig the graves. Anyone object to that?" Matt turned to Darin.

"I'll get the tarp," Darin said.

CHAPTER 10

Matt returned to the group, wishing they had a working faucet. He desperately wanted to wash his hands and get the smell of death off him. One of his neighbors from *before* hunted deer. Every year, the neighbor would hang his deer's corpse in the garage. On hot days, the smell would waft out, filling the block with a scent Matt couldn't describe other than death.

If Matt didn't get everyone buried soon, the same would be true for Camp New Beginnings. He guessed the ground would be thawed in the next hour and made a mental note to make that a priority. In the interim, it was time to make a plan.

"Can everyone gather around?" Matt asked. "We need to talk about what's next."

They all formed a circle around the remnants of the firepit. The rubble from the main cabin sat behind them.

"What now?" Kim groaned.

"Geez, Kim," Catherine said. "It's not all about you all the time."

"No, no arguing, please." Matt rubbed a hand over his buzz cut. "If you want to stay at camp forever or do nothing, fine. If you want to help, come join me over here. I can't take the fighting. I've had enough."

"What*ever*," Kim said.

Rhett put an arm around Kim and guided her toward Matt and the rest of the group.

"Let's break up into teams, okay?" Matt said. "Things have gotten real serious, real fast."

"You can say that again," Stacy said.

"Teams for what, chief?" Justin asked.

"We need to search camp for supplies," Matt said. "Go to all the cabins that didn't get demolished from the avalanche. And just like Darin suggested, we've got to be thorough. Anything and everything that might be helpful. Even if it seems weird, grab it. Let's check every cabinet and under beds. All the outbuildings and sheds need to be checked too. Whatever you find, bring it back here, so we have it all in one spot, okay? Pack it up, bring it here."

"What are we packing for?" Rhett asked. "Are we finally going to go to the mountain?"

"Yes," Matt said.

"Then gas masks are key," Darin said. "We absolutely need them."

"Great, fine," Matt said. "Everyone, please meet back here in the next hour or so, even if you're not done. Just to report, you know?"

"You mean make sure we didn't die?" Victoria asked. "That's the real reason, isn't it?"

Matt hesitated. "Split up. I'll see you all back here in an hour."

"I'll check the shed and any other outbuildings," Darin said.

"Lance-Darin, I'll help you," Stacy said, sidling up to him.

Kim rolled her eyes.

"Great." Darin blinked hard. "You guys got the cabins?"

"Sure," Justin said. "Cody, Victoria, and Rhett, you guys in?"

"Yes," Rhett said.

Kim frowned and pushed his arm off her waist.

"Sounds good to me," Cody said.

Victoria nodded.

"I'll check the infirmary, or at least I think it's the infirmary," Matt said.

"Count me in," Catherine said.

"All right, then," Cody said. "Kim, what are you gonna do?"

"Me?" Kim did a backbend and kicked her feet over. Her colorful pleated skirt fluttered and reminded Matt of every pep rally he'd ever been to. "I'm going to sit my pretty little butt right here and relax. Have fun."

"Kim, come on," Catherine said.

Kim sat on a log that had served as a bench the night before. "Come on what? Keep pushing me, and I'll make Rhett stay here and fan me. How about that?"

"No." Rhett shook his head. "I want to help. I have to find what's left of my family."

"Whatever." Kim rolled her eyes. "I guess you can go."

Catherine opened her mouth and hesitated.

"It's not worth it," Matt whispered in Catherine's ear.

Matt called back to his friends. "Hey, guys, try to find a place we can sleep tonight. One of the other cabins that didn't get destroyed."

"Sound good," Darin said.

"See you in an hour, chief," Justin said.

* * *

Matt led Catherine to a cabin on the edge of the avalanche chute. It wasn't much bigger than the other bunkhouses in this area of camp. To their right, Justin pushed his shoulder on a door, and entered a cabin. The door slammed behind him. Victoria followed Cody into another. They entered more cautiously than Justin, easing the door open and peering in first.

The door in front of Matt and Catherine had a white square with a chipped red cross painted on it. He turned the handle but was met with resistance.

"Is it locked?" Catherine asked.

"No," Matt said. "I think there's something blocking the door. Probably from the flood."

He turned to his side and thrust his shoulder into the door. It budged, but only an inch.

"Help me," Matt grunted. "On three. One, two, three!"

They took a small step back and slammed themselves into the door. It crashed open, and a chair flew across the small space, smashing into a doctor's exam table. Matt fell on his back; Catherine landed next to him on her side. He stared at her for a moment and tucked a tight black curl behind her ear. *Just like in the movies,* he thought. She smiled at him and held his hand.

"I'll be honest, that kinda hurt," Matt said, breaking the tension.

Catherine rolled onto her back and laughed. "This whole thing is so messed up, I'd expect nothing less. And hey, if you're injured, we found the infirmary."

Matt stood and stretched. Dusting himself off, he smoothed his filthy shirt. In the middle of the small room was an old exam table with a tarnished metal top. The table paper had long since been destroyed, but a thick, rotting cardboard spool from a roll still remained at the top. Across from it was a sink, soap, and two jars—one with matted cotton balls, the other with cottons swabs with long wooden handles. Below the countertop were four small drawers. Matt ran to the sink and lifted the faucet's handle.

Nothing.

He waited with his hands under the faucet, willing water to come out.

Catherine stepped up to his side and said, "We can go to the lake if you'd like after."

"Yeah, that'd be good."

Matt looked at her. Even in the physical state they were all in, dirty and bruised, he still thought she looked beautiful.

They held each other's gaze.

Catherine cleared her throat. "I'll check the cabinets under the counter." She opened a white metal cabinet on the opposite side of the table.

Matt shook his head and calmed his breathing. The

first drawer, just left of the sink, squeaked like a bike wheel void of oil.

"Are you finding anything?" she asked.

"Kind of." He scooped the contents out of the old drawer. "I've got Band-Aids, ACE bandages, and instant ice packs. You?"

"Some pills . . . um, this one says liquid iodine." She handed it to Matt. "And some Lortab and some antibiotics, I think."

The heavy, brown glass jar of iodine was still intact and didn't appear to have been damaged in the flood. She set the cloudy orange pill bottles on the counter next to him. He tilted them from side to side, ensuring they weren't one big, wet pile of pill mush. They'd work in a pinch.

"And scissors." Catherine dropped them on the exam table. "Arts and crafts in the infirmary?"

"No, those are hemo-something. I can't remember. Here, let me check something." Matt stepped onto the exam table and reached into the very top of the cabinet while Catherine moved out of the way. "If they're here, I bet there are needles and sutures too. Jackpot!" He held a plastic pack of curved needles and thread. "You may have just saved someone's life, Catherine."

"I had to have stitches in my hand once. It was not fun. The way the doctor pierced my skin—I don't even like thinking about it." She shuddered. "Did they teach you how to use those in Scouts?"

"Heck, no," Matt said.

"I don't want to be the guinea pig." Catherine smiled, and placed them in a green canvas bag she'd brought.

"Cody grew up on a farm and ranch. I'd bet a thousand bucks—if money mattered—on him knowing how to use them."

"I'll take that bet, Voorhees." Catherine held out her hand.

Matt shook it, then held on for a moment. "Uh, we should probably get back to the main cabin."

"Yeah." Catherine blushed and looked away. "Good idea."

Matt gathered up the rest of what they found from the drawers.

"Can we take a detour by the lake so I can wash off a bit?" Matt asked as they left.

"Sure thing," Catherine replied.

She looped her arm in Matt's and started to skip toward their water source.

Hopefully, everyone else had been this fruitful. Regardless, for the first time in a long time, Matt felt something strange.

Hope.

CHAPTER 11

As Catherine and Matt made their way back to the meeting spot, Justin came out from in between cabins.

"Hey!" Justin shouted. "Matt, you got a free hand?"

Matt stopped short and handed his canvas bag to Catherine.

"I'll meet you over there," he said, then jogged to Justin. "What's up?"

"Here, take these." Justin plopped a bunch of harnesses in Matt's outstretched arms. "I think it's for rock climbing. This camp must have been a pretty rad place back in its heyday."

"Schweet," Matt said. "Which cabin were you guys in? I'll drop these off and bring Catherine to help."

"Nah, this is the last load. We'll meet you by the firepit as instructed!" He saluted Matt then turned away.

The coarse harnesses dug into his arms while the carabiners clanked as he walked on the reddish-brown dirt. Surprisingly, glittery quartz rocks remained untouched and still lined the path perfectly, like some kid had glued them on a life-sized diorama.

Matt frowned at the damage once again. The main cabin was wrecked, along with a half dozen smaller cabins. All of the cabin roofs had become void of the moss that was so prominent when they arrived just a few days ago.

Matt adjusted the rope and climbing equipment on his shoulder. He figured they probably wouldn't be climbing the face of the mountain, but it was still a good find, nonetheless.

Piled next to Kim was a different kind of mountain. Stacks of hiking boots, carefully folded clothing—all army green—and tons of tools. Axes, shovels, and sledgehammers were the most common among the pile of tackle.

"Hey there," Darin said. "Nice find on the med supplies."

"Thanks," Matt absently replied. He picked up a crowbar. "Whoa, where did you guys find these? How the heck did we miss all of this?"

"Good question," Kim said. "Like, did you even try before?"

"Shut up, Kim," Catherine said.

"*You* shut up." Kim had her back against the supplies and was flipping through an instruction manual like it was the latest issue of *Seventeen Magazine*. "Seriously, Matt, some leader you are. All this junk was, like, at our fingertips, and you were only worried about dumb crap. Let's bury bodies, watch boring home videos, don't go swimming, I'm going to the truck," she mocked.

"I never said I was the leader," Matt said through

clenched jaws. "You're welcome to offer up suggestions whenever you'd like. That is, if you can pull yourself away from your afternoon nap, Madame."

"Princess," Kim corrected him, never looking up from her yellowed instruction manual.

"Anyway," Stacy said, "check out what Lance-Darin and I found. We made a really solid team." She winked.

She's a chameleon, Matt thought. She took on whatever personality granted her approval. He highly doubted her stories of being rich and popular. Whatever the case, he liked this version of her a lot more than when she hung out with Kim.

"We got these Special-K knives—"

"K-bars, not the cereal," Darin interrupted.

"And axes," she said, ignoring him. "Plus more shovels, flashlights, backpacks, these hideous clothes—and oh! We found an office! Check out the Trapper Keepers."

Stacy held out a Lisa Frank organizer with a rainbow background and a unicorn on the front. She lifted the top, and the Velcro ripped away from the bottom sticking to it. Plastic ripped a little and she shrugged.

The death of a Trapper Keeper, Matt thought. He knew it well. His last year of school, his had a red Lamborghini on the front, and it tore after the second week. Every time he pulled it out of his backpack, the top would fly open and papers would spill out. He finally resorted to using a large, blue rubber band to keep it closed.

"I searched the desk pretty good," Darin said. "Couldn't find anything that identified the owner of it. But we grabbed a bunch of these pencils, lead, and notebooks."

Matt examined the yellow Pentel mechanical pencils and gently shook one. The lead inside the walls of it bounced around. Aside from the yellowing pages, the purple notebook he held look brand new. He uncapped the eraser from the pencil and started erasing a line on the cover.

"This works better." Darin handed him a flat pink one with the words "Blackwing 602" scrolled across the front, printed in block letters.

"Thanks." Matt continued his work with the flat pink eraser until he had etched his name onto the cover. He grinned. "Sorry, I couldn't help myself."

"I used to do the same thing," Cody said, returning with Victoria.

"Did you cover your books with paper grocery bags too?" Victoria asked. "I always heard kids in the suburbs did that."

"Never did. Never cared," Justin said. "What kinda fancy school did you attend?"

"It wasn't fancy," she said. "It was just forbidden. Teachers would tear off any book covers and give you detention. We were required to keep our books pristine or else. No paper bag coverings. Looked too trashy, I guess."

They laid out more rock-climbing gear next to the pile of supplies.

"This is great," Matt said.

"Any gas masks?" Darin asked.

"No," Rhett said. "You said you found flashlights?"

"Yes. They're pretty old." Darin held up a bulky green rectangle with "Dyno Torch" embossed on the side.

"Squeeze the handle over and over and you create light. No batteries needed."

"Cool," Rhett replied. "We found compasses. I don't know how to use them."

"Not a problem," Matt said. "I can teach you. You don't have to be a rocket scientist to learn how." He palmed the round metal and watched for the needle to find a steady point. It bounced around, never stilling. "Hmm, that's weird." He tapped the compass's clear face. "It won't find a fixed point. Doesn't matter. I'll try the others later. Now that we've got our supplies, and more shovels, I think it's time."

"What about Kyle?" Victoria asked.

"As bad as this sounds, we're going to have to go search for his body. After that avalanche, who knows where it ended up and what condition he's in. And moving it might not be an option anymore," Matt said.

"Come on," Darin said. "Let's stick to this task first."

"Do we even, like, know where any of the corpses are?" Kim asked.

"Sadly, yes," Justin said. "We found them when we were searching the cabins. We used a couple bedspreads to drag them over to Nathan's body. Honestly, they were pretty bad. Skin falling off, completely bloated, the girl's arm looked like it had been ripped almost completely off her body and the smell—"

"No need to get to graphic," Cody said. "The point is, they're with Nathan and they've been wrapped in those blankets so no one else needs to see them."

"Everyone, grab a shovel or hoe. Let's do this together," Matt said.

"Even me?" Kim said.

"Especially you, Kim," Rhett said. "Nathan was my friend."

"Ugh, fine." She finally stood and toward the bodies. "Let's get these stiffs in the ground."

CHAPTER 12

Arguing ensued before they agreed to bury them by a crop of trees on the edge of camp. All in one grave. The girls stayed behind and dug while the guys dragged the bodies to the burial site. When Matt returned, Catherine, Stacy, Victoria, and Kim had made a decent sized dent in the grave site and were sweaty—all except Kim, who looked fresh as a spring daisy. Matt guessed she'd leaned on the hoe the whole time.

"Wow." Catherine gagged. "They're . . . fragrant."

"Yeah," Matt said. "Let's get this done quick."

He joined in the shoveling. After twenty minutes, his back ached, and his forearms burned. Sweat dripped down his back, making his shirt cling to him. It always looked so much easier in the movies. Even with nine people digging, it was slow going.

"Whoa!" Cody said. A loud clang followed. "Whoa. Musta hit a rock."

"We're almost done," Darin said. "Don't worry about digging it out. Just go around it."

"That's a hell of a stone." Catherine leaned over Cody. "Matt, check this out."

Matt wiped his brow with his forearm and stared down at an object with sharp angles. "Wait. That's no rock." His face twisted in confusion. "Is it metal?"

They chased the object down a few more inches. Matt jumped in the hole and scooped dirt out with his hands, excavating the artifact like a fossil from an archeological dig.

"Kinda looks like a jacked-up hubcap," Rhett said.

Matt dropped the piece of metal on the edge and climbed out of the hole.

"Weird." His face twisted with confusion. "It's a gear."

They all stood at the edge of the hole, staring down at a large, rust-colored gear.

"What do you think it is?" Catherine asked.

Matt knelt down to get a better look. He squinted. "I have no idea."

"Looks like someone just threw a bunch of giant junk out here to rust away," Darin suggested. "I mean, I saw a picture one time of a tree that grew through a bicycle, and several years later, the bike was about seven feet up and totally incorporated into the trunk."

"Yeah," Cody said, "that could be it."

They let an awkward silence settle in until Kim blurted out, "I'm gonna gag to death over here."

Matt turned and said, "Okay, I think this is deep enough. Let's bury them."

They grabbed the tops and bottoms of the tarp and blankets. Matt did his best to respectfully lower them into the grave, but his back strained, and it was too deep. He braced himself for the sickening thud the bodies made as they were dropped into the hole.

When Nathan, Dr. Westbrook, and girl number seven were all in the open grave, Matt said, "Anyone want to say a few things?" He suppressed a gag and pressed his index finger to his nose.

No one spoke.

"Okay—" he stammered.

"I'll go," Kim said, perking up. "The worms crawl in, the worms crawl out—"

"Kim, stop," Catherine whispered.

"The ants play pinochle on your snout," Kim sang. "Your stomach turns a moldy green, and pus comes out like whipping cream!"

"Kim!" Stacy shouted.

"What the hell's wrong with you?" Victoria asked. "Show some respect."

"What do you expect from me," Kim laughed. "I barely knew Na-Nathan and didn't know the other two at all. Sorry you froze up and got squished by beams? Sorry, scientist, for abandoning me in this hellhole? Sorry, girl who probably could have sold me some jeans at the Gap? I'm outta here. See you back at camp." She walked away.

"I don't know what you see in her." Matt turned to Rhett and shook his head.

"Maybe that's how she grieves," Cody said. "It's still extremely rude but . . ."

"I've got something to say!" Rhett blurted out. "Nathan, I'm sorry my girlfriend mocked your stutter. I really liked you and thought you were a big dork. But in a good way. I wish I could have saved you." He hung his head.

"Sorry, Nathan, and girl." Justin placed a hand on Rhett's shoulder.

"Nathan, I saw the look of fear in your eyes, the sound of terror in your voice. No one should lose their life like that," Victoria said. "Sweet girl, I didn't know you, and I hope you weren't panicked. We didn't get to you in time. And Dr. Westbrook, you gave up your life for us, thank you." She dropped a wildflower into the grave.

Catherine and Stacy followed suit and said a few nice words. Matt turned to Darin.

"I've said all I needed to say to Westbrook," Darin said.

"Dr. Westbrook," Matt said, "you did so much for us. Even up to the end when you gave your life so we could live—"

"He wasn't Jesus," Darin interrupted.

Matt continued, "I don't know if you had a wife and kids or what you left behind, but it's admirable. I'm so thankful I have a chance at a second life. Nathan, what can I say? You were great, and we all liked you. And girl number seven, I hope you didn't suffer."

Matt was the first to take a shovel full of dirt and toss it in the hole. It bounced off a floral comforter and rolled down the sides.

He looked to the group and nodded at them to do the same. After a few minutes, the hole was almost completely filled in. Soon, the only thing left was a large mound over the bodies.

"We'll need to make a proper marker for it when we

can," Cody said. "Wouldn't be right to have an unmarked grave."

"Now what, chief?" Justin asked.

"Would it be okay if I gave a crash course in compasses?" He took the one Rhett had given him out of his pocket. "This is so weird; do you have more of these?"

Rhett handed him two more.

Matt shuffled through the three compasses. "Okay, so maybe they got ruined in the flood, but they're all kinda working the same." The needles were going wild. They spun back and forth, never fixing on a given direction.

"I don't know," Matt confessed. "Compass class is canceled. I guess let's call where the truck wrecked north. The trail sort of splits the camp, the lake is east, and the mountain is south." He pointed. "That makes the main cabin just west of the pathway. Any questions?"

"What's the urgency to go?" Stacy said. "I'm feeling pretty sad."

"I made a promise to Kyle," Matt replied. "And the sooner we get him buried, the sooner we can find the cave and our families."

CHAPTER 13

Matt and the gang headed back to the collapsed main cabin.

"Me, Catherine, and Cody will go north, try to find Kyle's body, you know . . ." Matt said. "We can bury him at the truck once we find him."

"I'm good with that," Cody said.

"I just feel like we need to give him a proper burial before we go to the mountain," Matt said. "It's the right thing to do."

"Do you need help?" Darin asked.

"I think with the three of us, we should be good," Matt said. "We'll head to the mountain right after we get back."

"Okay," Darin said. "I'll get everyone packed up for the trek."

"Taking on the role of camp counselor already," Matt said, a tinge of sarcasm laced in his words.

"More like babysitter," Kim said.

Matt, Cody, and Catherine packed backpacks for

their day trip. Matt's bag consisted of a couple of cans of food, a knife, a canteen of water, and a wool blanket.

"Ready," Catherine said to Matt.

"Yeah, you got the supplies?" he asked.

"Yep."

Matt turned to the group. "Three hours max. We will be back."

"I'm, like, going swimming," Kim said.

"Figures," Matt said.

The three left their friends on the porch, walked down the red-brown dirt path, and passed the Camp New Beginnings sign that now lay on the ground next to the toppled archway. Matt looked back at the destruction the avalanche had done and held the bridge of his nose.

"You comin'?" Cody asked.

Matt jogged to catch up to Catherine and Cody, who held three shovels. Cody handed one to Matt.

"I'm so glad to have a break from Kim," Catherine said. "She's insufferable."

"I know it ain't right for a man to speak ill of a woman, so I'll just nod and say nothin'," Cody said.

"Sorry, not trying to gossip," Catherine said. "But I've had enough."

"Me too," Matt said. "Honestly, after her performance at the funeral, she can leave the camp. Too bad Rhett is so attached to her. We can't lose him, and he's actually pretty cool."

After twenty minutes, they had ascended the hill close to the truck. A deep scar of freshly churned-up dirt confirmed the avalanche had swept through the area. All smaller plants and scrub brush that had grown between the trees remained but had been trampled.

Then there was the truck. When they'd last seen it, it was wedged between two trees with Kyle's body propped against it. Now it was flipped upside down between the same set of trees. Painted white numbers and a letter stenciled on its undercarriage were now visible. The windshield was obliterated, the axles on both front and back were broken in half, and the driver's door was ripped off. Kyle was nowhere to be seen.

"Holy crap," Matt said. "How big was this avalanche?"

"That was no avalanche," Catherine said. "That was something else. It needs a different name."

"An apoca-lanche." Matt shrugged.

"I like it," Catherine said.

"Look at that." Cody walked swiftly toward the truck. "See this? We saw it a little bit when we was changin' the tire." He outlined the painted letters and numbers on the bottom of the truck. "B-35."

"Okay, we need to remember that," Matt said. "Don't know why, but I'm writing that down. We need to note the position of the truck, the painted number." He retrieved the Trapper Keeper from his backpack. First, he drew the location of the mountain and Camp New Beginnings. Then he sketched a rudimentary image of the truck: two circles under a rectangle. On the rectangle, he wrote "B-35," then scribbled the question: *What does this mean?*

"Man, I thought the truck was toast from the flood,"

Catherine said. A stump had wedged into the radiator. "Look at it now."

"It's gonna be hard findin' Kyle," Cody said.

"Probably," Matt said. "Let's get searching."

He and Cody fell silent.

"I mean . . ." Catherine's eyes darted side to side. "I just—I'm not blaming anyone. But Nathan and Kyle—I don't want anyone else to die."

"I know what you mean," Matt said. Still, he felt such guilt and overwhelming responsibility for both losses. The pit in his stomach grew as he worried about what the future held. They'd have to be extremely careful and watch each other's backs. "Let's stick together instead. I think the best bet is to follow the avalanche chute. It probably carried his body off. Maybe just fan out like ten feet apart from each other. We should be able to cover more ground that way."

With Catherine to his right and Cody to his left, he walked and used the shovel to push away the damaged foliage. He'd done something similar when he earned his search and rescue badge, never expecting to actually use the learned skill. They explored in awkward silence for half an hour before Matt paused to wipe his brow. The only thing they found was a couple halves of the cryo-pods. The lining had been torn out, and the padding spilled out, soaked with melted snow. The other half was cracked, and a portion was missing, leaving the pod a jagged heap of broken plastic.

"This feels weird," Cody said. "Like we should be callin' out his name or somethin'."

"Makes me sad," Catherine said. "What if I'd climbed

up just a second or two quicker? Then Matt could have helped Kyle. That's all it would have taken."

"You can't blame yourself," Matt said. "If it's any-one's fault, it's mine. He was scared, and I was yelling at him. We did the best we could. Who would have predicted a flood and avalanche like this? We need to be on guard. And guys, you know we're not finding his body, right? It's long gone."

"Matt," Catherine said.

"Now just wait a goll durn minute," Cody said. "You didn't create the rain. This is no one's fault. It was an accident. Trust me. I've been down this path with my brother."

"I forgot," Matt said. "I'm sorry."

"No sorry needed." Cody swung his shovel, mimicking Matt. "I blamed my brother for bull riding—a stupid sport, I might add. I blamed the bull, who was just being a bull. Heck, I even blamed God. Let me just tell you, none of that made me feel better. In fact, I felt worse. Kyle's gone, and that's that."

Matt shook his head. "You're right, and thank you. I need to stop making it about me and blaming myself. Look over there, see it? What is that?" Matt pointed to his left. "Something is shimmering over there."

CHAPTER 14

Cody chopped through thick scrub with his shovel and ran ahead toward the glinting object. Matt sprinted closely behind. Ferns whipped Matt in the face, but he put it to the back of his mind and forged ahead. He looked over his shoulder and saw Catherine following right behind him.

The small group came to a skidding halt. Matt stumbled into the back of Cody, and Catherine ran into both of them. Before them was an enormous gray metal door hanging on hinges that were mounted into granite stone. Embedded in the door was a square window reinforced with diamond-pattern silver wire.

Matt took a deep breath of the thick, sweet-smelling, humid air. "What the . . ."

A generous hill loomed in front of them with a seemingly random door in the forest beckoning them to enter. Overgrown brush and tree branches hung over the door, concealing most of it. But the sunlight hit the window just at the right angle, exposing its location.

Matt cupped his hands on either side of his eyes and peered into the glass. "I can't really see anything. Looks abandoned."

"Is it a cave?" Catherine asked. She knocked on the door. Matt jumped back.

"Geez, you could've warned me." Matt rubbed his forehead.

"Sorry," she said. "Just thought it was worth a try before we do a little B&E."

Matt pulled down on the metal handle.

"Locked." He jiggled the handle harder this time. "What do you guys want to do? We can keep searching for Kyle, but I think he's long gone. Or we can see what's in here. I'm guessing we've only got about an hour, maybe an hour and a half before we need to head back to camp."

"I dunno," Cody said. "I feel terrible givin' up. But I think you're right."

"Well, if you two are on board, let's commit the 10-62 and get past this door," Catherine said.

Cody removed his backpack and rummaged around, producing the Dyno Torch flashlight. "Guessing there ain't a generator in there."

"This could have the answers for us. Heck, this could be the entrance to the cryovault!" Matt said.

"Don't get your hopes up," Catherine said. "Dr. Westbrook drove us out of the cryovault. Remember the video? And there's no way a truck is fitting through that door."

"There may be a truck entrance somewhere." Matt grabbed a rock and hit the door handle. "I don't know.

It's something. It's gotta be. If someone took the time to build into a hill, completely conceal it, and lock it, then there's something big behind these walls."

Matt dropped his canvas bag and produced a hatchet. "Watch out."

He lifted the hatchet over his head and swung, connecting with the window. Vibrations stung his forearms, but he kept swinging. The futile attempts of trying to break the window didn't even leave a crack.

"I guess we'll have to do this the hard way." Matt raised the small ax again, but this time came down on the handle.

Catherine took the map from the Trapper Keeper in Matt's bag and started scribbling on it. "What should we call this place?"

"How about Hillside Bunker?" Cody asked.

Matt's hands ached with each blow to the handle. He was doing no favors to his recently injured wrist. But the handle was no match for the hatchet, and it finally gave. It fell to the forest floor amongst a bed of leaves. The only things left were holes where mounting bolts were inserted and a spring that protruded from the larger hole where the inner hardware for the handle was. Matt cleaned the chipped metal debris and spring from the hole and felt around with his finger. Pressing the small metal latch past the strike plate, he thrust the heavy door inward with his shoulder.

"Ready?" Matt said.

Cody and Catherine nodded.

Matt sucked in a sharp breath and shivered. He stepped through the threshold and was hit with the unmistakable odor of chemicals. Coconut sweetness of gamma-nonalactone and the strong fruitiness of isoamyl acetate encompassed with hints of the pungent rotten-egg aroma of sulfur.

Memories of high school chemistry lab flooded his mind.

Simpler times for sure.

"Ugh," Catherine said. "That stings my eyes."

"What is this place?" Cody grabbed a chair from a stack propped against the wall and wedged the door open.

Outside light flooded in from the open door. In what looked like a small reception area were six black steel drums with a skull and crossbones stenciled across the front in white paint. Across from that were two plastic blue barrels labeled "Potable H2O" with curled-edge stickers.

Matt ran to the blue barrels. He rubbed his hand over the sticker, then knocked on the side.

"Could it still be good?" Catherine asked.

"If it was properly sealed, it would be," Matt said, shaking a barrel. The liquid sloshed around inside. "This looks legit. I had these old neighbors, nicest couple I ever met—they were Mormon—and they stored water like this."

"Why?" Catherine asked.

"I dunno." Matt used his canteen to wash off a two-sided, cloudy-white corrugated hose. "Something with their religion and storing food and water . . . for the apocalypse." Matt laughed. "I didn't really ask much after they told me that. Besides, I was there for the lemon meringue pie, and let me tell you, it was the best I ever had. When we find my mom, please don't tell her I said that."

Matt unscrewed the white lid and sniffed the liquid inside. "Smells like water. Whatever water smells like."

He snaked one side of the hose into the hole and screwed an orange siphon onto where the cap had been. Cody pushed and pulled the pump's lever up and down several times until water sputtered out, then streamed with each time Cody depressed the handle.

Matt rinsed his hands in the liquid, then cupped his hands underneath, letting it pool. He sniffed it again and dipped the tip of his tongue into it.

"How is it?" Catherine asked.

"Tastes a little bit like plastic, but better than the lake water," Matt said, lapping up the rest. "Give me a little more. I'll drink it, and if I don't get sick, we'll know it's good."

"Good idea," Catherine said. "This is a game changer, guys. How big is that barrel?"

"Fifty-five gallons of glorious H2O," Matt said. "Okay, I'm going to put this on the map. Let's see what else is here."

There was a spot for a desk, but if it had been there, it was long gone now. In the middle of the room was another metal door with the same stenciled writing as the truck: "NO ADMITTANCE A-67."

Matt checked the handle. To his shock, it turned. Cody pumped the old flashlight, giving them a steady beam of yellow light. Catherine held the door and propped it open with a chair just as Cody had done.

"Last thing I want is to get locked in here," Catherine said. "We can't take any chances."

Cody walked to the center of the room and spun in a slow circle, casting light on the darkened areas. The windowless room was fully inside the hill. It was at least twenty degrees cooler than outside. Six butcher-block black lab tables were evenly spaced apart. Atop them were forgotten Bunsen burners and beakers with crusted chemicals in the bottom, flasks turned on their sides, and graduated cylinders of varying sizes.

"Looks like someone had been conductin' experiments and abandoned it midway through." Cody picked up a flask and held his flashlight up to it.

"Dang." Matt held his nose. "Guess we found the source of the smell."

Mounted to the wall on the right side of the room were an eyewash station and an emergency shower. Matt recognized both from his high school days. He had been tempted to pull on the long triangle handle whenever an unsuspecting classmate stood under the large showerhead, but never did.

"Why is there a lab in the middle of the forest, buried under a hill?" Catherine asked. "Was this like a nerd summer camp?"

"Maybe," Matt said. "Could have been a multipurpose summer camp. Sports for half the summer, then academics in the other half."

"What's with all the No Admittance and locked doors if it was just for a summer camp?" Cody asked. "I ain't never heard of a camp that specialized in both school and sports. Course, I only ever went to church camps."

"Good point," Matt said. "I don't know why all the secrecy and the numbers A-67 and B-35. I got it all written down. Cody, what's piled up over there?"

"Looks like them cryopods." Cody crossed the room.

On the opposite wall of the eye wash were three older-looking pods. Matt rushed over to them.

"Looks like gen one," he said. "Definitely older than ours."

Matt searched the outside of the pod, looking for a release handle. The surface was rough, and the overall shape was less egg shaped and more pine-box-coffin shaped. His palm located a lever. With a swift turn to the right, the cryopod clicked. The corroded plastic lid snapped and creaked under the strain. Hinges that probably hadn't been used in years resisted Matt lifting the lid. With some effort, he swung the lid open.

"Shine it here," Matt said. "Whoa, look at this. Are these feeding tubes?"

Inside the rectangle was a raised bed like Matt had in his cryopod, but it wasn't nearly as plush. Crusty yellow tubes and exposed wiring lay in a tangled bundle.

"Glad we weren't stuck in those," Catherine said. "They look like a prototype or something."

"Rhett never would have fit in there," Cody laughed.

"For sure," Catherine said.

"This is weird," Matt said. "Why would the pods be here?"

"I'm freaked out," Catherine said. "This is creepier than the Fratellis' basement."

Matt and Cody both laughed at her *Goonies* reference.

"Let's hope Sloth isn't hiding down here," Matt said.

"Honestly, though," Catherine said, "I could go for a Baby Ruth right now."

Matt walked back across the lab. "Baby Ruuf."

"Head down that a way," Cody said, shining the flashlight.

Another hallway jutted off the other side of the lab. Four doors lined the hallway. Two on one side and two on the other, all metal, all painted drab green. Matt turned the handle to one, revealing an office.

"This is like breaking into the principal's office," Matt said. "Almost feels like we need a lookout."

Cody handed the flashlight to Catherine. "Wanna give it a try? My hand needs a break."

"Sure." Catherine took it from him and began pumping the handle. She shined it on a large bank of shelves behind the desk. "I wish we'd brought the lantern."

The modestly plain office had a desk in the middle with all the usual suspects. Decades of dust covered the metal "mail in, mail out" tray, stapler, boxy computer in the middle, and tape dispenser.

Propped up against the desk was what looked like a movie poster secured with a rubber band. Matt slid off the rubber band, which disintegrated in his hand, then he unrolled the poster-like paper and laid it out over the desk, covering the computer keyboard. What stared back at him was faded blue-gray paper with dark blue lines. At the top, it had a red rubber stamp on it. *TOP SECRET* and A-67.

"Blueprints," Matt said.

CHAPTER 15

They gathered around the desk and stared at the blue-prints.

Matt traced the outside of a mountain with a small entrance noted at the base. He turned the extra-large paper over and saw the plans for a warehouse inside the cryovault. The warehouse had a large opening—large enough for a bus—and gradually, the building led down.

"Holy shi—" Matt dropped the blueprint and took a step back. "Guys, this is it. These are the blueprints to the mountain, the warehouse, and the cryovault!"

"Does it say where?" Cody asked. "It's gotta be nearby."

Matt flipped a page. "No, not that I can see."

"A-67 . . . is that what it's called?" Catherine reached in front of Matt. "See, it's on the top of every page. That must be what the site is called. A-67. And what's this? Why are the words at the bottom blacked out?"

"We can't see. You're hogging all the light," Cody said.

Matt and Cody huddled around her like she was holding the flashlight and telling a scary story.

"Look, the cryopod columns—this is what we saw in Dr. Westbrook's videos." Matt pointed. "So assuming this is cryovault A-67 . . . then we're not alone."

"Not alone?" Cody asked.

"I'm following ya. The truck said B-35." Catherine twisted her thick curls into a knot behind her shoulders. "This blueprint is for cryovault A-67."

"And the truck has B-35," Matt interrupted.

"Exactly," Catherine continued. "So we must've come from cryovault B-35."

"For sure!" Matt punched the air.

"No way." Cody shook his head.

"Yes way," Matt said.

Catherine rummaged through a metal tray. "See this?" She held up a piece of letterhead. The top right corner had black marker with lines over it. "It's redacted. Just like on the blueprints. They only do this for serious stuff, you guys."

"Let's not get ahead of ourselves." Matt approached the bank of cabinets. "We are for sure onto something. We need to do a good search of this office and the others."

On the back wall of the office were three robust steel closets. Matt yanked on the handle, and it barely budged.

Gears screeched off in the distance.

The ground tremored slightly.

Everyone paused.

Catherine gripped the edge of the door frame as if she were in an earthquake. Matt locked eyes with her before ducking under the desk.

"Ya'll heard that, right?" Cody asked.

"Yeah." Catherine nodded. "I hope it's nothing. But maybe you should find a doorway or something."

Matt felt his heartbeat in his ears.

Pound! Pound! Pound!

If it was another flash flood, they'd be trapped inside the hill. One way in, one way out. Drowned.

Like Kyle.

Matt knew he needed to Matt-itate, but finding anything to focus on seemed impossible. He swallowed hard. "Co-Cody, can you run out and see if anything is happening?"

"Ten-four," Cody said.

Matt heard Cody's footfalls become more distant. "Catherine, are you okay?"

"I should be asking you the same. This—whatever it is—is traumatizing. I can't live in constant fear."

"It's just so, I don't know, unpredictable." Matt emerged from under the desk. "Sometimes it's something, and other times it's nothing. Or at least nothing here. Maybe the weather is bad far away."

"Nothin'," Cody said, running into the room. "Everything seems to be right as rain."

"Well, that's a relief," Catherine said.

"For now," Matt mumbled. "Thanks for checking, Cody."

"Glad to help."

"Time's a wasting," Catherine said. "Let's see what's in the cabinets and bounce."

Matt shrugged. He planted his feet and pulled with both hands. The closet hissed as he broke the sealed connection, revealing its contents. Catherine shined the yellow flashlight beam on floor-to-ceiling boxes.

"Jackpot!" Matt exclaimed.

Organized neatly were hundreds of white boxes with black print that simply said "Potato Chips" across the front. On the bottom, it stated if they were plain or flavored and that there were two packages per container.

"Open one. See if they're still edible," Cody said.

The top of the box was sealed like a cereal box, and just like every other time Matt had tried to open one, he accidentally tore it, ensuring it'd never close right again. Inside were two small silver pouches. He pulled the seams apart, and the aroma of greasy potato chips caused his saliva glands to fill his mouth with spit. The chips looked perfectly preserved, albeit generic.

Matt turned one over in his fingers, inspecting every inch. "They're not black, so that's good."

Cody rolled up the blueprints. Matt dumped the chips onto the desk.

"No bugs," Catherine said. "Seems good. Who's going to try it first?"

No one budged, but Matt licked his lips.

"Oh geez," Catherine said, then popped one into her mouth. "Holy crap, these are fresh."

"The cabinet, it was sealed," Matt said. "They must've preserved all of this. Open the next one."

Matt and Cody opened separate cabinets at the same time. Matt's had "Vanilla-Filled Sponge Cakes" and "Chocolate Cream-Filled Cakes" in them.

"Twinkies and Ho Hos?" Matt shrugged. "Don't mind if I do."

He tore into the knock-off Twinkies and handed one to Catherine before greedily shoving a whole one into his mouth.

"Oh, Twinkies, you really did withstand the apocalypse," Catherine giggled.

Cody presented them with movie theater-sized boxes of various candies simply labeled "Chocolate" or "Non-Chocolate." They opened one, and inside were individually wrapped red spheres. Cody indulged first, and his face turned deep red.

"Atomic Fireball?" Catherine asked.

"Yep." Cody spit it into a trashcan. "Too hot for me."

"Try and reseal the cabinets," Matt said.

He pushed on one. When it clicked, a stream of air released from all four sides, like when his mom would "burp" Tupperware.

"Okay, last one. Any guesses as to what's inside?" Matt pulled on the door.

"Gum?" Catherine said.

The cabinet was split into two columns. One side had white cylinders with black print that read "Cheese-Fla-vored Balls." On the other side were hundreds of white aluminum cans labeled "BEER."

"Wow," Cody said. "Didn't expect that."

"Me neither." Matt resealed the door. "Let's see what's in the other three offices. Hey Catherine, you still creeped out?"

"Buzz off," Catherine said. "The junk was good, but it just raises more questions. Why is it here? Why are there sealed cabinets?"

"Maybe they were planning on waiting it out here,"

Matt said. "We all knew the apocalypse was inevitable. Heck, they froze *people*. Why not ensure there are food and supplies for when they defrost them?"

"Defrost?" Catherine laughed. "Now you're starting to sound like Darin."

Catherine led them into the second office, where the desk was barren, but the cabinets revealed similar nondescript, black-and-white boxes of dried meats. Most were normal, like chicken and beef, but there were more exotic ones like alligator and ostrich. Cody said he'd had alligator jerky before and claimed it was pretty good.

Matt took over with the flashlight duties for the last two offices—if you could call them that. The office in the back corner had no desk but a cabinet full of freeze-dried vegetables. A shiver ran up Matt's spine.

"Let's hurry with the last one and get out of here," he said.

"Bets on what type of food we'll find?"

"Dairy?" Cody guessed.

"Got that covered in the cheese balls," Matt said.

"Grains is my guess," Catherine said.

"Oh, I hope so," Matt said. "I'd love some toast—it's probably my favorite food. Lots of butter and honey, or with cinnamon and sugar, maybe some peanut butter."

"Toast is your favorite food?" Cody yanked a cabinet open in the final office. "I woulda guessed pizza."

"It *is* bread!" Matt said when he saw inside the cabinet. "Pita bread, but hey, that works."

From top to bottom were white boxes that read "Flatbread." The one next to it housed "Nut Butter" and "Fruit Spread." Catherine tore open a box. Inside were small pouches. In the last two, they discovered "Thin Pasta" and "Tomato Sauce." The sauce was in the same packets as the peanut butter. Matt guessed it was a better way to store it over canning.

"Okay, let's grab some PB&J, maybe some chips, and head back to camp for dinner," Matt said. "This is a great find! Once we have everyone, we can move some supplies back to the cabin. But I think it's best if we keep them sealed up here. It's not a bad walk, maybe thirty minutes?"

"Do you think we can trust the others?" Catherine asked. "Like, Kim won't come up here and steal all the Ho Hos?"

"What can we do if she does?" Cody asked.

"True," Catherine said. "I just worry this might . . . I dunno. People can get weird with resources."

"I'm not gonna lie about it," Matt said. "Remember how pissed Justin was because we didn't tell him about the canned goods in camp? I just got him on my side, sort of. I hope we can just all be a team and not screw anyone over."

"All right." Cody walked out of the beam of light. "Lead us out of here. I'm with Catherine. This place is a little creep-tastic."

CHAPTER 16

"Wait," Matt said. "What's that?"

He shined the light on a brown legal file pocket. Next to it were a few papers, as if someone had left in haste. He picked it up and headed for the exit. Once outside, he removed the black rubber string that secured the large flap.

"I think we should name it the Research and Development Lab instead of Hillside Bunker," Matt said. "Or R&D for short."

"I was thinking 7-Eleven, or the Sev, like me and my friends used to call it. But R&D is good." Catherine removed several packets of peanut butter from the top of her bag before extracting her Trapper Keeper. Then she smoothed the paper and clicked her mechanical pencil a few times.

"I'm cool with the Sev," Matt said.

Cody raised his hand. "I vote for that as well."

Matt thumbed through the file, expecting more papers. What he found were pictures.

"Guys." He dropped to the ground and splayed out the fading Polaroids. "Construction pictures."

"No way!" Catherine dropped her pencil on top of the map and abandoned it for the time being.

"Look. The truck." Cody shook the picture toward them. "ARMY CORPS OF ENGINEERS" was stenciled on the side of the green construction vehicle. "This is military. Our government built the vault."

"Well, I mean, I figured that," Matt said. "It wasn't like we had any time to prepare for this. Some guy in a black suit showed up at our house, talked to my parents, and told us to be ready for transport in three days. I always assumed it was the government."

"Right," Cody said. "But now there's no mistaking it."

"Not just military." Catherine stood, her hands trembling. "Demo Trench. See? These workers, their orange vests say 'Demo Trench.' They hired a private company. We now know there are at least two cryovaults—A-67 and ours, B-35—both inside caves, inside mountains. They must have taken years to build. How did they keep this a secret?"

The ground lurched, and gears scraped against metal. Matt paused and looked around frantically, but nothing happened.

"Same way they kept Roswell secret. And JFK's killer," Cody said. "Everyone in Texas knows Lee Harvey Oswald didn't do it on his own. Tarnished the whole state's reputation."

Matt thumbed through the pictures. He saw huge excavators moving dirt and rock. Then equipment was hauled in on flatbeds of semis. Steel beams and rods that made up the columns were shiny and free of rust.

"Come on," Matt said. "Let's get back to camp. It's starting to get dark, and I want to see if Darin knows anything about this. Maybe Dr. Westbrook mentioned it to him."

They hurried back to camp while keeping their eye out for Kyle's body. Guilt tugged at Matt. He'd promised they'd come back and bury Kyle right after he'd died. Matt hoped they'd get the chance to search again, but knew he needed to resign himself to the fact that they might never recover him before they left to go to the mountain. He had to stop letting the guilt get to him.

"It feels like we're so close, but I have more questions than ever," Matt said. "I miss my parents. I just need to see if they're okay."

"I know," Catherine said, stepping over the New Beginnings sign. "We all do."

The rest of the group sat on the wraparound porch of the main cabin.

"What the . . .?" Matt said. "Guys, am I hallucinating?"

"No," Cody said. "It's—"

Catherine shook her head. "Unbelievable!"

"I've got no words," Matt said.

"You guys rebuild the cabins or what?" Cody yelled toward the group.

"No!" Darin answered. "It was like this when we got back."

He stood as Matt, Catherine, and Cody approached.

"Wait! What?" Matt asked. "The main cabin just reconstructed itself?'

Darin stretched his arms out wide. "That's what I'm

saying. You didn't see anyone else that could have done it? And I'm telling you we didn't do it. It was fully erect when we got back from our walk."

Matt shook his head. He couldn't believe what had happened. It made zero sense.

"Where did you go?" Matt asked. "I thought you guys were going to pack?"

"We went on a walk," Justin said.

"I needed a break from the cemetery," Stacy said.

Justin rested against the railing of the porch. "You're not going to believe what we found!"

"Huge, big metal things," Rhett said.

"What are you talking about? Like equipment?" Cody asked.

"No, like gears. Like the guts of a machine. But a gigantic machine," Justin said.

"It was totally lame," Kim said. "I could have been attacked by a bear. And it was really sweaty."

"Not now, Kim," Matt said. "There's a what? A huge machine?"

"No, just parts," Justin replied.

"You can let these two brainiacs try and tell you, or you can apologize for being rude, and I'll explain it," Kim said.

"Sorry?" Catherine said. It came out as a question.

"I meant them." Kim pointed at Rhett and Justin. "Anyway, there are, like, these gears and junk like that. Did you ever see the cover of Queen's *News of the World*? Not the cassette, the vinyl."

"Yes." Matt shook his head. "Why does that matter?"

"Like, my parents always played that crap to torture

me." Kim twirled her hair. "It has this huge, ugly, metal-looking giant on it. In his hands are dead people he's crushed. It looks like that bald weirdo destroyed a giant car or something and hurled the gears into the ground."

"Can someone tell us what's really going on?" Catherine rubbed her temples.

"No, she's right," Justin said. "There are enormous pistons and fans and hydraulic arms just—I don't know—plunged into the ground. I've never seen anything like it."

"Okay, wait," Matt said. "Start over. Darin, what is going on?"

"Listen." Darin stepped in front of Matt. "You gotta quit asking me that!"

Matt relented. "I understand. Okay, so why did you leave camp?"

"I needed to get away from the grave," Stacy said, raising her hand. "Like, mourn, you know? I asked them all if we could just go on a little hike or something to, like, get the thought of Nathan and stuff out of my mind."

"So you went on a hike . . . and what?" Catherine asked.

"Like I said," Justin replied, "enormous gears and junk. A junkyard made from giants."

Rhett cleared his throat. "I've never seen anything like it. Kim is kinda right. It's just like that record cover."

"We didn't even tell you the best part," Justin said. "We found some cargo trucks! We tried to start them, but they were dead. Cody, you're good at fixing crap. Do you think you could get them running?"

"What!" Matt exclaimed. "This could change everything!"

"No guarantees, but I'll give her a try," Cody said.

"That's an amazing find," Matt said. "Let's go. We might even be able to find the cave tonight."

"It's almost dark," Justin pointed out.

"He's right," Cody said. "I need full light to see what I'm dealing with. Plus, they might be solar. *Hopefully, they're solar.*"

"Right. We'll go at first light then," Matt said. "But tell me about the elephant in the forest."

Justin raised an eyebrow. "Huh?"

Matt pointed to the main cabin. "What's the story with this?"

"Like I said, they were like this when we got back," Darin repeated.

The main cabin and all the other bunkhouse cabins that were destroyed by the avalanche were put back together. Fully erect.

"Are they safe to sleep in?" Catherine asked.

"I don't, like, see any avalanches in the distance, do you?" Kim asked. "Stay outside if you want."

"I'm exhausted," Matt said. "We have a big day tomorrow. But for now, let's eat."

"Great, more weird-tasting, metallic food," Victoria said. Then she sighed. "I'm sorry. I shouldn't be so negative."

"Girlfriend"—Catherine wrapped her arm around Victoria's shoulder—"what if I told you we had some peanut butter and jelly sandwiches with a side of chips with your name on it?"

CHAPTER 17

The group settled into the cabin for the night. After the sun went down, it cooled off dramatically. Catherine filled the rest in on what they'd seen and found north of camp at the R&D lab.

"We're calling it 7-Eleven, or the Sev," Catherine informed them.

"Sounds wonderful," Victoria said. "There's really all that food?"

"Yeah," Catherine said. "And it's not too far from here."

Justin lit a fire while Matt unloaded and portioned out sandwiches and chips for everyone. Victoria and Stacy filled a large pot with water from the lake.

"Let me." Darin took the water from both girls. "Justin, you ready for this?"

"Give me one sec." Justin propped up a metal grate above the fire for the pot to rest.

"While we wait, let's gather around, if that's okay," Matt said.

Folding chairs were set up as they readied to eat. Rhett's chair creaked as he took a seat next to Kim.

"I can't believe you found food," Darin said. "Oh, this jelly is so sweet. Peanut butter's a little weird. Tastes like the almond butter they had at the cafeteria in school."

"Whoa." Matt held out his free hand. "No one said *peanut* butter. Just nut butter."

"So weird," Kim said. "My parents would have never bought this garbage."

"No one is forcing you to eat it," Catherine said.

Kim placed her half-eaten pita bread on the ground next to her feet and crossed her arms.

"Don't mind if I do." Justin plucked it from the dirt.

"Sick," Kim said under her breath.

"I grew up on this stuff. Government commodities," Justin said. "And look where being a snob got you: a seat right next to me. Only difference is my belly is full. Mom used to make Tuna Helper when things were tight—which was most of the time. It was so gross, yet so good at the same time. I'd give anything for her cooking."

"Sick!" Stacy laughed. "That makes me want to gag just thinking about it. Canned tuna, blech! Although, speaking of tuna, I could go for some sushi. My dad, he used to take me once a month. It was our thing, you know?" Stacy's voice cracked and she cupped her hands over her face.

"We'll find them." Victoria rubbed Stacy's back. "And you're right. Sushi is the best. We had so much good food in Manhattan. When my parents bought the apartment above us, they renovated both apartments into a two-story home. They cooked so rarely, they got rid of both kitchens." She laughed. "We only had a mini fridge and wet bar."

"No way," Kim said.

"Believe what you want. It's actually pretty common. No one in the city cooks—too much goodness around every corner."

"Do you think we'll ever have something like that again?" Catherine asked.

Matt didn't think so, but he wasn't going to say it.

An awkward silence filled the room.

"I wish we still had the TV." Rhett changed the subject. "We found a few older movies in one of the cabins."

"Me too." Victoria smiled.

"Whatever!" Kim shot to her feet. "I'm going to sleep."

"Hang on, babe," Rhett said. "I want to hear what Matt's plan is."

"Oh yeah, right. Guess we got sidetracked," Matt said. "Here goes. And I'm open to suggestions."

The fire flickered in the background, and all eyes were on him. For the first time, he admitted to himself that he was the leader.

"As you know, we all really need to head to the mountain and save our parents and siblings. Let's call that south. But I want to check out the junkyard as well. That can be east. So I say the plan for tomorrow is to pack up some supplies here, go east to the junkyard, and on the way to the mountain, we can swing by the Sev, which is a little north, and get lunch supplies and more gear for our trip to the mountain. Sound good?"

"I'm good with that," Catherine agreed.

Matt looked around the room.

"Isn't the Sev far from here?" Rhett asked.

"Yeah," Kim said. "The less sweating, the better."

"It's not too far," Cody said.

Rhett shrugged. "Okay, then."

"Did I tell you there are Twinkies?" Catherine asked.

"Yeah, a whole closet full of junk food," Matt said. "It's food heaven."

"That's it?" Victoria asked. "Junk food?"

"No, no," Catherine said. "There's all sorts of food, dried veggies, and bread." She held up her sandwich. "It seemed like we could get a well-balanced diet and no metal taste."

"Awesome," Justin said. "I can't wait. Then off to the mountain."

Everyone seemed to be on board. After dinner, Justin, Rhett, and Cody went to the cabins unaffected by the avalanche to retrieve more blankets and sleeping bags. The ones they had set up for the other nights were soaking wet. After everyone settled in to go to sleep, Matt approached Darin with the folder of Polaroids.

"Hey, Darin, can you explain these?" Matt handed Darin the brown file folder. "What do you know about construction of the cryovaults? Did you know there were multiple vaults?"

Darin opened the file folder and stared at the pictures, dropping each into his lap.

"I was a tweenager when they froze me." Darin stood. "Sorry to disappoint you, but they didn't trust top secret info with a kid."

"Fine. Fair. I'm not accusing, but you were awake for

years," Matt said. "Dr. Westbrook never told you about other vaults?"

"No."

"Did you guys go to the other vaults to take care of those people?" Matt asked.

"I told you I didn't even know about them."

"I assume there are other scientists, like Dr. Westbrook? And other pods?" Matt asked.

"I have no idea," Darin said. "I have the same information as you. Hey, why do you think there's other cryovaults?"

Matt pulled the blueprints from the backpack by his chair. He unrolled them and said, "See here in the corner, stamped, it says 'A-67.' These are blueprints for, I assume, a vault A-67. The truck we came in on has 'B-35' all over the undercarriage. Painted on. So I assumed that these pictures and these blueprints are for a vault A-67 and that we must've come from vault B-35."

"Wow." Darin clapped Matt on the back. "Watch movies much? That seems like quite a stretch."

"Well, that's what it means." Matt vigorously rolled the blueprints, annoyed.

"Listen, Westbrook probably didn't even know how the caves were built or if there were others. He only cared about making sure his people lived so he looked good."

Or that the entire human race didn't die out.

Darin gave the folder back to Matt. "And what do your pictures prove? That it was constructed? Big whoop." Darin threw his hands in the air. "We all knew that. Do you think the cryocolumns just spontaneously appeared inside a cave? And are you really shocked there are other caves? Five thousand people isn't very many. I always assumed there were multiple. That way, if one failed—like ours did—the human race would still have a chance. Ever hear of not putting all your eggs in one basket?"

"What about the breach?" Matt tilted his head to the side, remembering what started the whole thing.

Darin stiffened.

"The one you were awake for," Matt continued. "The one that affected our column."

"I—I don't know. Meteor, I guess," Darin said.

How does he not know? He was there. They fixed it with carbon foam.

Dodgy answers like this frustrated Matt. Normal questions were met with vagueness or non-answers. Matt bit his tongue, while his suspicions about Darin spiraled.

"Lance-Darin," Stacy called, patting the floor next to her.

"Look, I'm on board with your plan," Darin said. "I absolutely want to find my parents too. I do. But it's not going to help them if I die in the process. So we need to be smart about this. I like the idea of getting more food for us. We have all the gear we need. We will need to carry water."

Matt took a deep breath and slowly released it. "Yeah, you're right. I'll see you in the morning."

"Yeah." Darin yawned. "See you tomorrow."

Matt crawled into his sleeping bag on the hard floor. The fire died down as he was faced with his own thoughts and guilt. Sleep was fleeting that night. He stared at the rafters of the massive A-frame. His eyes followed one cable to an eyelet as big as his fist, where the end was secure. In the other direction, the cable coursed through two pulleys and down to a bolt where the end was fastened.

Could those be why the cabin sprung back up? he thought, scratching his head.

"No, I didn't know! I didn't mean to. I didn't know what I was doing!"

Matt knew that voice.

Darin.

Matt tiptoed toward him and stared at the sleeping man.

"You're crazy." Darin thrashed from side to side in his sleeping bag. "You did this. It was a trick. I'm sorry. Please, no. No! Don't put me back in the pod!"

Darin's entire body tensed then relaxed. Matt watched him for a few minutes to see if he'd say anything else. Once satisfied the sleep-talking was over, he returned to his own sleeping bag.

Now for sure he couldn't sleep. His mind was reeling about what Darin had said and how the cabins in New Beginnings were reconstructed.

Repositioning over and over, he couldn't find a comfortable spot. Once he finally fell asleep, he had dreams about his parents—that he'd found them trapped in their cryopods. Frozen in death, their eyes wide with shock, like Kyle's had been.

His body jerked, pulling him from the nightmare, before his eyes fluttered closed once again. The Kyle nightmares began with his second wave of sleeping. Kyle army-crawled across the rugged terrain. Something was wrong with his legs, and they dragged behind him at unnatural angles. He kept calling out Matt's name. Begging him for help. Matt's own legs were encased in jagged lava rock, and he couldn't do anything. Kyle inched closer and closer. Then a flash of lightning ripped across the sky. Kyle's face was contorted, cheeks hollowed out, eyes deep set, and his lips dripped with blood. Kyle smiled wide—far too wide—and said, "You're next." Then he jumped to his feet with his hand outstretched toward Matt.

"Ah!" Matt sat up in his sweat-soaked sleeping bag.

He looked around the room, thankful he was the first one up so no one heard him cry out. The sky filled with dim light and brightened up the gym. Matt stared at a piece of peeling varnish on the floor and did his Matt-itation. His breathing and heartbeat slowed, returning to normal. Darin stirred in his sleeping bag, then rolled onto his back.

"Darin," Matt whispered. "You up?"

He nodded but didn't open his eyes.

"Meet me on the stage. Help me with the packs."

"Nightmares?" Darin hopped up onto the stage.

"Yeah," Matt said. "You?"

"Every night," Darin said. "I don't think I'll ever shake the ghost of Westbrook."

"I heard you talking in your sleep," Matt said.

Darin sorted through items, never looking up or responding.

"You kept apologizing, saying you didn't mean to. What's that about?"

"Living with, or rather under, Westbrook's rule was torture. I don't want to get into it, okay?"

"But what happened? What didn't you mean to do?"

"Nothing." Darin stared at the floor.

"You keep getting mad because I don't trust you, but you keep giving me reason not to," Matt said, trying to keep his voice even.

"It was—look, I can't. It was the worst trauma of my life. Shit went down and I had to—no, please. No. I'm not ready."

"How can I believe you when you keep hiding things?" Matt felt heat rise up in his chest.

"Do you want to relive the worst thing that's ever happened to you? Did I make you go into detail about how Kyle died? Blame you? No!" Darin's face was red and he was panting. "It happened. *All* of this has happened. We were all pawns in some weird game where Westbrook was playing both offense and defense. I know you don't believe me, but I will tell you—just not now."

Matt paused. He saw how upset Darin was. Whatever happened to him must have been really bad. Or he was hiding something really big. But Darin was right, this wasn't the time. "Let's just get everyone a backpack, okay?"

"Fine by me," Darin said.

"I think we just need to pack light—compasses, first aid, things like that," Matt said, shifting the conversation. "We can get food at the Sev."

"Fine," Darin said. "You distribute those. I'll pack some ropes, MREs, and whatnot."

"Cool, cool—"

Gears popped, and a small tremor shook the floor.

The rest of the group shot to their feet.

"Ugh," Kim said. "Nice wake-up call, Matt. Like, are you trying to put me in a bad mood?"

Matt said nothing and rushed to the nearest window. The sky was clear. He ran to the window near the front and watched the mountain.

But nothing came.

"Come on," Matt said. "Everyone grab a backpack on the stage. If you're up to it, take a hatchet, hammer, ax, or even shovel. Justin, you lead the way."

"All right, chief. Hold your horses," Justin said. "Let me drain the snake first."

"Disgusting!" Stacy said.

"No breakfast?" Kim asked.

"Do what you have to do, I guess, and let's meet at the lake in ten minutes. *Everyone.*" Matt glared at Kim. "Also, I'd suggest getting some new clothes on. More for protection. Cheerleading uniforms and dresses might not work."

"Screw you, Matt!" Kim said, stripping off her sweater and dropping her skirt. She strolled over to the trunk in her underwear. "You're such a jerk. I will always be a cheerleader!"

"Kim!" Stacy said. "Like, inappropriate."

She shrugged, throwing clothes in the air, searching for something that fit. "I don't care anymore," she pouted.

Matt turned away.

"I'll help you." Rhett stood between her tiny frame and the rest of the group, blocking them from her tantrum.

"Yeah," Kim said to Rhett, "I know."

Victoria cautiously approached the trunk, not knowing how Kim would react.

"You think I'm good, guys?" Stacy asked.

"I think so," Darin replied.

Rhett dropped his trousers and slipped into a pair of gray sweatpants. He took his T-shirt off and put on a mesh football jersey.

Catherine grabbed a pair of Guess jeans and a pale yellow *Return of the Jedi* shirt with three-quarter sleeves. She exited the gym to a room off to the side. Victoria quickly snatched up youth army-colored cargo pants and a black Billy Idol concert tee.

"Can I come with you?" she asked Catherine.

"Absolutely," Catherine answered. "I'm not as daring as Kim."

Catherine and Victoria returned within a few minutes. Kim, on the other hand, was taking her own sweet time. She held up a T-shirt, then tossed it onto the pile of clothes. She held a pair of jeans to her waist and shook her head.

"You good?" Rhett asked.

"Yeah," Kim replied, "just trying to find the perfect outfit."

"This isn't the first day of high school," Darin finally piped in. "We really need to hustle."

"Fine," Kim said. She slipped on white Jordache jeans and a purple top. Then she held her hair down with a lime-green headband. The white Kaepas with gold and blue triangles on the side completed the outfit.

"There you go!" Kim said. "Like, how do I look? Ugly? Horrible?"

Matt walked across the gym to the front door of the cabin. "Good enough, Kim." He was at his wit's end. He'd lost his patience for her a long time ago, and they had only been together a few days.

Matt set his backpack on the porch and took a deep breath. He rummaged through his pack once more, making sure he had everything he deemed necessary for their survival. Everyone was taking leaving the camp seriously. Matt could hear Kim asking Rhett if she had everything she needed. Hopefully, his annoyance and the gravity of the situation were sinking in.

Victoria left for the lake first. She sat on the dock, feet dangling above the water. Matt joined her on the old wooden dock. The water seemed lower than usual.

"How are you holding up?" Matt asked.

"I was just about to ask you the same thing." Victoria stared at the water.

"Me?" Matt raised his eyebrows.

"You've been the one taking the brunt of everything." Her long black hair, still in a frizzy plait from yesterday, hung lazily over her shoulder. "How are you coping?"

"I . . ." Matt paused. "I honestly haven't had a chance to think about *how* I'm doing. Okay, I guess." A hitch caught in his throat.

"You're strong, not like me." Victoria stood and smoothed her T-shirt.

"Stop—" Matt started.

"But we all have different strengths, and that's what makes us stronger together. Isn't that what Kyle said?"

"Yeah," Matt said. "Something like that."

"I see people. *Really* see them." She closed her eyes

and tilted her pale face and upturned nose toward the sky. "Read people well, you know. Kyle was more than a Young Republican. He was eager to learn, unafraid to make mistakes. That's what I liked most about him. Nathan also wanted to learn, be better, but he was paralyzed with fear over letting you down. That's what made it so much worse when he died. That frozen look on his face wasn't terror. It was knowing he'd let you down in the worst way, Matt."

"I-I didn't know," Matt said. "What else do you see?"

"I'm not judging, Matt. Just observing," Victoria said. "Stacy wants to be liked. Craves it, really, and she'll conform to whoever's personality to gain it."

"Yeah, I can see that," Matt laughed. "She acts so different now that she's trying to get approval from Darin."

"Justin and Kim are the most similar. It's striking, really. They're both damaged, just in different ways. Kim was ignored, showered with gifts to make up for the neglect. Parents who bought her love. The only thing handed to Justin was a slap to the face after being cussed out."

"He said that to you?" Matt's eyes grew wide.

"No. He didn't have to." Victoria pursed her lips. "Kim and Justin both claim to not care and push everyone away, Rhett withstanding. Isn't it funny that they're both drawn to him? Justin wants to be a good guy, but sometimes he just can't help himself. He wants to heal and create a new life. Rhett is exactly what we all see. Easy, unassuming, and wouldn't hurt a fly."

"What about me?"

"Matthew Voorhees, you aren't as strong as you look.

You're stronger. You just don't know it. Not yet. But you will. Come on. The others are arriving. I'll fill you in on the rest later."

Matt hadn't realized how thoughtful Victoria was. He had looked at her as sensitive, if not weak. This was his first time one-on-one with her, and he regretted not doing it sooner. He wondered what she saw in him that he neither saw nor felt in himself.

CHAPTER 18

They spent twenty minutes trudging through the under-brush, following Justin and Rhett, and Matt only counted seventeen times where Kim complained about something.

"It's just over here," Justin said. He jumped over a large tree trunk and landed unsteadily on his feet. "Careful, the ground is slick."

Matt opted to climb over it and take his time. His wrist finally felt better, and he didn't want to risk re-injuring it. Or worse.

"Holy . . ." Cody said.

"Wow!" Catherine exclaimed. "What is this place? It's like we shrunk."

Kim's description had been spot on—even though Matt was reluctant to admit it. Among the bright green, overgrown grass and dark green shrubs were enormous pieces of a machine unlike Matt had ever seen. Untarnished hydraulic arms plunged out of the ground and soared twenty feet into the air. Matt counted six enormous gears. It was like being on another planet. He climbed up in the middle of a gear and held his arms out-stretched.

"Dang," Matt yelled, his voice sounding like he was in a tin can. "I can't even reach either side of this baby." He jumped to try to reach the top.

"What are these things?" Stacy asked. "It's like that movie *The Incredible Shrinking Woman* that came out a few years ago."

Matt hopped up onto a smaller gear that was lying on its side. "Whoa, Stacy," he said. "I didn't see you as the movie type."

"Well, I'm just going off the title," she giggled.

"I think this is a piston," Darin said. "A giant piston. Westbrook showed me a couple mechanical things like this. Out of one of the broken-down trucks. This is crazy."

In the center of the mess was a twelve-foot-wide, six-foot-high metal casing with a long, shiny pole slid into the center. At the top was an eyelet. It reminded Matt of his dad's beer opener.

In between the pistons were flasks and beakers on 'roids.

"These things are huge." Cody pressed his face against the side of the oversized chemistry glassware. Residual gray and brown water filled them three feet high.

"I bet all six of us could fit inside that beaker," Stacy said. "Lance-Darin, did you bring a ladder?"

"Nope," he said. "Just an ax."

Matt pulled himself up onto another gear to get a better vantage point. Off to his right was a metal fan bigger than his childhood home. It made no sense. Just like everything else at Camp New Beginnings. Next to it was a cart of some sort.

"Guys, come over here. I think I found something," Matt said.

"Is it, like, more trash in this junkyard?" Kim asked.

"Come on. I'll give you a piggyback ride," Rhett said.

Kim tiptoed toward Rhett, and a small smile formed on her lips.

A tram of some sort was on its side, and a pile of tracks were in front of it. Pine needles and dirt were piled in the bottom of the carts. The tram had three cars that sat cockeyed. Its vinyl-covered benches had torn, and the mustard-yellow stuffing was rotted out of them.

"These look like really unsafe rollercoaster cars," Matt said.

"Why would they be out here?" Rhett said.

"Why is any of this here?" Justin clapped Rhett on the shoulder. "Why do people pin and cuff the bottom of their jeans? Why did the Bears make a Super Bowl Shuffle? Where *is* the beef? Life is just full of mystery."

Pop!

Grind!

Screech!

Matt swallowed hard and turned his attention to the sky. Dark clouds formed south of them in the direction of the mountain. To the north were big, white puffy clouds.

"I don't get it," Catherine said. "This place looks like a giant took apart a car and left it to rust in the forest.

"It doesn't explain the oversized chemistry set or that fan," Victoria said. "Someone, or *something*, put it here, and I'll bet it wasn't a giant."

"Let me know when it's time to go," Kim said. "Come on, Stacy, let's see if we can find some flowers for our hair."

"I don't know." Stacy turned to Darin.

"Why are you looking at me?" Darin's eyes moved nervously from side to side. "I don't care what you do."

"Oh, okay." Stacy's face fell.

"Hey," Justin's voice echoed. "Guys, the trucks are over here!"

"Finally, isn't that what we came here for in the first place? Like, get me outta here," Kim said. "Justin, yell again so we can find you."

"Marco!" Justin's voice called out from behind Matt.

"Polo!" Catherine sang back.

They climbed over smaller machine parts and around the enormous ones until they found him.

"Look, they say 'Demo Trench' on the side," Justin said. "They must've dumped all this stuff here. Has anyone ever heard of these guys before?"

"Demo Trench was on some papers we found at the Sev." Matt shifted. "Don't know why. We'll show you when we get there."

"Well, the truck's had better days," Victoria said.

"What the heck, Justin?" Kim kicked a flat tire. "This hunk of junk hasn't run in, like, decades. This isn't going to get us to the mountain any faster than if we walked."

"But maybe we can fix it?" Justin asked.

"I doubt you guys can fix this one, Cody." Darin poked his head under the bed of the truck. "Rims are bent, axle is destroyed, and I doubt we'll find any gas or oil for it. But maybe the others?"

"Way ahead of you." Cody poked his head up from under the green, rusted hood of a cargo truck. "We had to piece things together on the ranch some days. Town was far—an hour round trip. I'm pretty good at robbin' from Peter to pay Paul. If anyone knows what a radiator line looks like, see if you can find an intact one on another truck."

"You're on your own, buddy," Justin said. "Not my forte."

"Mine either," Matt said. "These trucks remind me of that movie *Commando*."

"That movie was sick!" Rhett said. "A bunch of guys from my football team snuck in to watch it."

"Ah, yes," Matt laughed. "The forbidden R-rated movie. My dad took me, made me swear I wouldn't tell Mom."

"Your dad sounds like he was cool," Rhett said.

Was. Past tense. Matt's heart ached.

"Anyone find me a radiator line?" Cody asked.

"Sorry," Matt said. "I wouldn't know what I was looking for."

"Not a problem." Cody walked from truck to truck, peering under the hoods. Jostling wires, pulling and prodding. "This one seems to be the least rotted. Give me a few minutes and I'll know if I can salvage it."

Matt stared at his friends' faces. Each wore a different expression of anticipation or anxiety. If this didn't work, they'd wasted an hour and were no closer to finding the cave.

Cody hopped into the driver's seat and left the door ajar. "No one get your hopes up, but it's worth a shot."

Matt watched him turn the key, expecting to hear the truck struggle to life. But instead, he heard nothing. Not even the clicking of a dead battery.

"Damn it," Justin said.

"Let me check one more thing." Cody jumped down and lay under the vehicle. "That's odd . . ."

"What?" Darin asked.

Darin looked under the truck again along with Cody. "It says 'HZRD' on it. We've seen this before."

Matt swiftly grabbed the trapper. "HZRD, you say?"

"Yup," Cody said.

Matt scribbled on his map and took notes. B-35, A-67, HZRD. "Nothing makes sense."

The sound of gears revving up filled the air. The ground shook. Stacy grabbed onto Darin, who surprisingly didn't shake her off.

"Uh, excuse me," Cody said. "This ain't good."

"No duh. The truck is, like, useless. And what's with your stupid hick ain't bull crap?" Kim mocked. "Ain't ain't a word. And you ain't supposed to say it. If you say ain't five times, you ain't going to heaven."

"I wouldn't joke about that right now." Cody pointed to the sky. "Those clouds are about to collide, and we're looking at something bad."

A fierce gust of wind ruffled their clothes. A sudden cold bit at their skin. Black and white clouds swirled together, creating a deep gray overcast. Lightning streaked across the sky with a loud crackle. Another jagged bolt struck a tree nearby. Sparks jumped, and the tree smoldered. The clouds churned. Deep gray funnels riddled with electric bolts formed to the south until one stretched out like the devil's finger.

"Twisters!" Cody yelled.

"Run!" Justin shouted.

"No!" Cody held out his hands. "You can't outrun a tornado. They're unpredictable and faster than you can imagine."

"What do we do, then?" Matt said. He strained to hear Cody over the vicious squalls of air.

"We need to lie in a ditch or low area." Cody searched around desperately.

"There isn't a ditch!" All color drained from Victoria's already pale face.

"Then over here. Follow me!"

Cody ran toward a gear in the outer area, away from the glass flasks and beakers. The large gear was half stuck in the ground at an angle, creating a semi-shelter. Matt sprinted, but the wind had gotten stronger and pulled at him from every direction. He lost his footing, stumbling onto the hard ground.

"Matt!"

Someone's faint voice called his name.

Matt rolled over onto his butt and stared into the distance. A huge, mile-wide mass spun on the ground, picking up everything in its path and adding it to its deadly vortex. A tree was sucked up and spit out in sharp, thick splinters. Dirt and grass swirled in the black tornado. He froze at the sight. Someone yanked his shirt. He shook his head and half-sprinted and was half-dragged to the closest thing they had to safety.

"Are you trying to get killed?" Justin dropped him in a heap with the rest of the group.

"No, I . . ." Matt's chest tightened.

His breath came out in short spurts. He'd frozen just like Nathan. Matt's heart raced.

"Matt?" Catherine gently rubbed his back.

"I'm . . . okay," he stuttered. "Ju-just give me a sec."

Matt stared at the rusty brown surface of the gear and tried to Matt-itate. He counted to ten and back in his head.

"You better calm down, or you're gonna pass out, chief," Justin said.

Matt puckered his lips and slowly sucked in a deep breath, then closed his eyes. The air tasted moist, like petrichor after a rain. But there wasn't any rain. He thought about when his dad taught him to ride a bike. He'd been nervous then, but it was different. That was exciting. The air blowing through his brown hair. The instability once his dad removed his hand from the seat. The uneasy wobble that he managed to recover from. The purple and white streamers fluttering on the handlebars of his borrowed bike. "Once you prove to me you can ride, we'll get you your very own bike." His dad's words echoed in his head. All of it. Every moment calmed him and filled him with warmth. He blinked his eyes open to everyone staring at him.

Everyone but Victoria. She hadn't followed Cody.

CHAPTER 19

Matt stared at a small, pale, fragile girl, hunched under a downed tree. Her braid had come free, and long waves blew sideways across her face as she struggled to hold on. Her eyes were wide and filled with fear.

She yelled something to the group, but it was swallowed up by the ravenous, blowing wind.

"What happened to you?" Catherine asked, cupping her hands around Matt's ear.

He did the same to her. "I just had a freak-out for a second."

"Yeah, don't do that agai—" Catherine looked past Matt, her eyes wide.

Matt turned. The sky birthed hundreds of tornados. Some stayed up high; others lapped at the ground like a thirsty dog to water. At least half of the weather monsters connected with the earth, chewing up everything in its path. Cody had one thing right: They were unpredictable. The vortexes would shift and disappear, only to reappear closer to them. One sucked up a huge beaker, sending glass shrapnel everywhere. Matt ducked just in time to see the vortex being pulled back up into the sky as if it had satisfied its craving.

Victoria scrambled on all fours until she was out in the open. Exposed to the storm. She paused for a moment, looking back over her shoulder, then bolted toward the group. The fierce wind whipped her around, but still she trudged forward.

"Victoria!" Matt yelled, holding up his hands like a traffic cop. "Stop! Get out of the open!"

Broken branches clawed at her, knocking her around like a rag doll. She stood and tripped on a downed branch. Her green cargo pants tore from the thigh down. The fabric whipped around like a paralyzed appendage.

A piece of glass lifted off the ground and sliced into her leg, but she didn't falter. Bright red blood streamed down her thigh, a sharp contrast with her white skin.

Matt started and stopped over and over, weighing the risk to run out and help her, to pull her back in, to carry her. Anything to get her to safety. He was wrestling with what to do when, in a flash, the choice was taken out of his hands.

Rhett pushed past Matt, knocking him to his knees. He raced into the open area.

"Rhett! No!" Kim yelled, but her voice was swallowed up by the raging tempest.

Victoria's already shocked eyes somehow got wider. She trudged toward Rhett, her head down. The wind was too powerful for the thoughtful, delicate girl. A gust, swelled with dirt and leaves, hit her with the force of an oncoming bus. She was down, crawling. She outstretched a hand toward Rhett. The blood from her leg was stolen by the storm.

Intense pressure built in Matt's ears, so he pressed his palms into them. It felt like the world was going to explode. A deeper gray cast them into darkness. The sound of a freight train without the warning of a horn took Matt by surprise.

Rhett ducked.

Victoria didn't.

The broken-down truck they'd seen lying lifeless was now on a collision course. It spun violent and unpredictable in the tornado's funnel, tumbling over and over. Everyone screamed. Victoria stood and tried to run, fighting intense wind, unaware of what was chasing her. The truck flipped in the vortex just before its wheel well smashed into the back of Victoria's head. Matt ducked instinctively. Although the tornado was deafening, he swore he heard the sickening thud as it connected with her.

"Victoria!" Catherine screamed.

She took a step forward, but Justin grabbed her by the waist. She turned and buried her face in his muscular chest. Matt wanted to look away but was powerless. Dirt and leaves smacked him in the face, but his eyes remained fixed.

Victoria's head rolled toward them.

Eyes.

Hair.

Eyes.

Hair.

Eyes.

Her decapitated body remained upright for a moment then slumped. Blood poured down from her neck, leaving a crimson puddle around her body.

Matt's jaw slacked. Before he could fully process what had happened, the twister swept up what remained of their sweet, considerate, sensitive friend. He looked away.

"We gotta get Rhett!" Kim ran out toward him. "Rhett!"

Her baggy purple shirt wrapped around her slender body as she fought the wind. She fell and lay with one arm outstretched, her mouth agape.

"Come back!" Kim screamed, barely audible over the gale-force winds. "Please."

Then she was still. Completely unmoving. Rhett turned toward Kim, and he was hit with forest debris in the back. His large-statured body jolted and jerked like it was being shot, but he didn't fall.

Everything slowed. Motion and time didn't seem to matter.

"Get back here now!" Cody yelled, knocking Matt back to reality.

The force of the wind made it seem like Rhett was stuck in thick swamp mud. His face contorted. Another piece of debris connected with his shoulder, he lurched forward, and grimaced. Lightning tore through the sky, exposing hundreds of tornados that grew from the dark clouds.

"This is bad," Darin said. "Something's wrong."

"No shit, Sherlock." Tears streamed down Stacy's face.

"I—" Darin turned to Stacy, gently grasped the back of her neck, hesitated, and kissed her. Stacy's face reddened.

Then Darin ran to Kim.

"Lance-Darin!" Stacy yelled.

He was knocked back by a gust.

"No!" Stacy screamed. "Please, no."

Darin sat and pulled Kim toward him. Kim kicked at him. In one motion, he stood and placed his arms around Kim's waist, then heaved her over his shoulder. She pounded his back with closed fists in protest. He stood and ran back toward the gear.

"I gotta help Rhett," Justin said.

"No," Matt said. "It's too dangerous!"

Rhett dropped to his knees, then fell face-first onto the ground. A thick piece of jagged metal stuck out of his back. The storm had turned him into a wind-up toy. To never be wound again.

Even with all the commotion, wind, and tornadic activity, Matt still heard Kim's shrill cries over it all. She kicked her legs wildly but was no match for Darin. He ran hard against the wind and was only a few feet from the safety of their shelter.

Rhett pushed himself up and attempted crawling.

Darin ducked under the gear and dropped Kim onto the ground. He pointed at her and said, "Stay!"

"No!" Kim screamed.

Catherine and Stacy held her in their safe place.

"I can't take this." Justin ran toward Rhett but stopped suddenly.

A new funnel cloud snaked its way toward the

ground, ready to strike Justin. He backed up and dove back under the gear, skinning his forearms. The skinny tornado quickly quadrupled in size and devoured everything in its path. It launched another piece of debris at Rhett, but he was prepared this time. He raised a massive forearm and blocked it, fileting his skin open in the process.

The twister then shifted its path and started to circle Rhett. Like a boxer sizing up its opponent. The rest were powerless. The choice to help was not theirs to make anymore. If Matt or anyone else left the sheltered spot, the risk was too high for both to survive. Matt had never felt such guilt in his life. His friend was only fifty yards away, and there was nothing he could do.

The tornado slowed and swirled in one spot, throwing up dirt in every direction. Rhett attempted to stand once again. He took one step, then two steps forward, but then, like a cobra, the tornado struck, sucking their 6'6" jock away, hurling him up into the sky.

Matt closed his eyes and focused on his breath. A collective gasp and scream echoed behind him. Kim's cries were unmistakable. He'd never heard such pain or agony come from anyone or anything. She lay on her back, Catherine and Stacy at her side. Clear snot dripped from her nose; tears streamed down her bright red face as she struggled to get free from the girls.

"Rhett!" Kim cried. "No, no, no, no, we have to help him!"

Catherine stroked Kim's blond hair. "He's gone, Kim. I'm so sorry."

"Rhett," Kim wailed. "This is all *your* fault. You did this!" She stared at Matt like a crazed animal.

Matt Voorhees snapped.

CHAPTER 20

Matt's temples throbbed, and his entire body felt hot. He ground his teeth and flared his nostrils. Kim wasn't the only one who had just lost someone. They'd *all* lost Rhett and Victoria. In the last few days, every single one of them had experienced the loss of four friends, a scientist who took care of them, and a girl they'd never known. And now Kim was assigning blame to Matt. It was more than he could take.

"Shut your damn mouth!" Matt yelled. "You're so selfish, Kim. This isn't about me or you—it's bigger than us. No one is to blame. I didn't create that storm! I didn't force Rhett to chase after Victoria!"

The storm slowed, and the winds died down. Everything felt eerily calm.

Kim turned to Cody. "You should have stopped him!" she screamed. She glared at Justin. "You should have helped him, Justin. He was your friend. And where were you?" She pointed to Darin. "Why didn't you save Rhett? You should have just left me out there!"

"Kim—" Stacy started.

"No." Kim swiped Stacy's hand off her shoulder. "You're just as guilty. What? You didn't want to mess up your stupid red hair? So you just stood by and watched him die?"

"We lost Victoria too," Catherine said. "I'm sorry, Kim. We all are."

"Shut up!" Kim stood.

"Stop this!" Stacy shook Kim. "Listen, like Matt said, it was Rhett's decision to run after Victoria. Rhett is a hero. That's why he tried to help her."

"You're so stupid, Stacy," Kim said in between sobs. "No one cares what your idiot mouth has to say."

Stacy's face fell flat. She raised an eyebrow and put a hand on her hip. "Is that so? First of all, my hair is strawberry blond. *Not* red. And maybe, just maybe, Rhett tried to save Victoria because he liked her more than you."

"You bitch!" Kim slapped Stacy.

Stacy held her cheek, stunned.

"Okay, that's enough! No one talk!" Matt said. "Kim, you especially should use this time to grieve. And be silent."

Kim's legs gave out, and she collapsed into a puddle of tears.

"He could still be out there," Cody whispered to Matt. "I've seen it on the news before. Someone gets swept up into a twister, and they find 'em alive and well two towns over."

Kim looked up at Cody with glassy eyes. "What did you say? You're stupid too. He had a piece of metal sticking out of his back. He's dead, you moron. Dead!"

"You know what? Ima listen to Matt and seal these lips." Cody put his hands in his pocket and looked toward the sky.

Matt sat with his knees up to his chest. He thought about how he'd barely had time to grieve the loss of Kyle and Nathan. Now he had to add Victoria and Rhett to the list. Four lives—four kids, really—who had survived the apocalypse, cryosleep, and a car accident only to die by the natural disasters that made it necessary for cryosleep to be invented in the first place. His friends had succumbed to the natural disasters. Rain, snow, and now wind.

Mother Nature was a murderer.

Catherine sat next to Matt. She leaned over and rested her head on his shoulder. "You know no one blames you, right?"

Matt shrugged.

"Matt, come on, be reasonable. Look at her." Catherine nodded in Kim's direction. "She's a mess. Hurt people hurt people. It's easier for her to hate us than deal with her feelings."

"I guess." Matt stared at Kim. She quietly wept in the fetal position, in utter grief. "I'm just tired of being her punching bag. I shouldn't have yelled at her. I feel terrible."

"Then apologize," Catherine said. "But you weren't out of line."

"Thanks for saying that." Matt hugged Catherine. "The sky is still dark, but it seems like the weather has lifted."

"Do you guys want to try to head back to camp?" Catherine asked. "We need proper shelter."

"The wind is starting to pick back up," Darin said. "It might be our only chance to run for a while."

"There still might be bad weather at camp," Matt said. "But at least we'd have more cover in a building. Not getting hit with debris every few seconds."

"I'm in," Justin said. "Should we leave it to a vote?"

"Nah," Cody said. "If you want to stay, stay. I'm leaving."

"I'm in," Matt said.

Catherine nodded.

"Me too," Justin said.

"Camp sounds good to me," Darin said. "It's only a thirty-minute walk, and if we run, we can make it there in no time."

"I trust you, Lance-Darin." Stacy weaved her arm through his.

Darin stiffened. Matt guessed he regretted kissing Stacy.

"Kim," Matt said, crouching next to her, "I'm sorry for snapping at you. Will you come with us? We can't leave you alone here."

"Rhett's gone," she cried. "Nothing matters anymore."

"It's getting pretty windy," Catherine said. "It might start up again. This is our only chance."

"We can't leave her," Matt mouthed.

"Scoot aside," Darin said. He picked Kim up and placed her over his right shoulder. "If you won't walk, we'll carry you."

Kim lay limply over Darin, still crying.

"Let's go." Matt jogged out from under the gear and was immediately hit with the earthy scent of moist air. He didn't see any tornadoes, so he waved everyone forward. "Stay in a group, but let's get there as fast as we can."

"I'll lead," Justin said.

"Thanks," Matt said.

Matt found his place firmly in the middle. Thirty minutes passed. Kim protested and said she'd run. But every time Darin placed her on the ground, she would just lay down and cry. With all the starts and stops, it was taking them longer to get back to camp than it did to get to the junkyard in the first place.

"Get up or be carried," Catherine said. "Kim, I know you're sad, and you can cry and grieve all you want once we're in the main cabin, okay? You can stay there for the rest of your life if you want."

"What's the point?" Kim rolled over into a puddle of mud, staining her purple shirt and white jeans.

"The point is you're hurting all of us right now," Matt said. "Get up, or I'll carry you."

Kim stood and shuffled her feet. She flat out refused to cooperate.

Is she trying to get us killed? Matt wondered.

While Matt wasn't the strongest, he decided it was his turn. He scooped her up and held her like a baby, her muddy clothes staining his. She struggled at first, kicking her feet and flailing her arms. Matt briefly considered dropping her but thought better of it.

"Give me your hand," Stacy said to Kim.

Matt gently deposited Kim back on the ground, his back protesting the entire time.

"I'm sorry for what I said," Stacy said. "And I know *you're* sorry for slapping me. Run with me, Kim. Please."

Kim wiped away a tear, smearing mud on her cheek in the process. She gave a single nod and lazily ran, hand in hand with Stacy.

CHAPTER 21

Kim's improved attitude didn't last long—not that Matt expected much of her. She'd tripped over a log, and she lay on the ground crying, Stacy at her side. Branches creaked, and leaves rained down on them as the winds picked up once more.

"Come on, Kim," Cody said. "I ain't ever yelled at a lady in my life, and I'm not about to start now. But you have got to either run or let us carry you. This is getting so dang frustrating."

"I'm so sad," Kim said. "I've been, like, traumatized."

"We've *all* been traumatized," Justin said. "Enough is enough. Cry later. We're all hungry, tired, and cold."

Darin clenched his fists and stalked back toward Kim.

"Move," Darin said to Stacy.

Stacy jumped to her feet and out of the way. Darin crouched and scooped Kim up and over his shoulder once more.

"This is the last time I'm doing this," Darin grunted.

"No!" Kim protested.

Darin held her over his shoulder and clamped her thighs down with his left arm. Leaving his right arm free, he jogged. Matt matched his pace and ran next to him.

"Can you bring up the back, Justin?" Matt asked.

"You got it, chief," Justin said. "No soldier left behind."

"Let me down!" Kim pounded on Darin's back. Tears streamed down her red face. "You're kidnapping me!"

Kim's mud-stained feet flailed while she screamed. "I hate you!"

"You know what? I'm done." Darin said. "I can see the lake from here. I'm not screwing with this anymore."

He put Kim down. Kim kicked Darin in the crotch.

He doubled over. Matt could only imagine the flames of nausea coursing through Darin's gut after a kick like that.

"Kim!" Stacy yelled. "Did you kick Lance-Darin in the—the—you know?"

"He deserved it!" Kim wiped tears from her face. "He dropped me . . . again."

"Whatever!" Stacy chased after Darin. "We've tried everything. You're being completely ridiculous. Friendship over, Kim. Friendship over!"

Matt looked back. Kim was, once again, on the ground in the fetal position, sobbing. Catherine crouched next to her and held her hand.

Leaves whipped at their feet in the swirling wind. Matt waved Justin and Cody ahead.

"Come on, Kim. We're not leaving you," Matt said.

"Good luck, chief," Justin said. "Kim's being a real shit-eating brat right now."

"Tell me about it," Matt replied.

"We might just want to leave her, as hard as that is to say," Cody said. "Matt, she's slapped Stacy—twice, and punched Darin in the ole family jewels. Just because she's a girl doesn't mean she's allowed to hit us."

"You're right." Matt rubbed his face. "I just need to get her back to camp and have her chill out before I address it, you know?"

"Tick tock." Justin tapped his wrist on his non-existent watch.

Matt nodded and gritted his teeth. When it came down to brass tacks, Matt wanted to leave Kim in the woods. He figured she'd come running like a toddler whose parents threatened to leave them in a store during a tantrum. But he couldn't leave her to just die. She'd been hand-picked for the cryovault program just like himself. If nothing else, he'd do it for Rhett. His friend. His dead friend. He squeezed his eyes shut and pushed back tears. *Not now, Matt, deal with it later.*

Matt approached Catherine and Kim, who was now standing.

"Kim has agreed to come with us, as long as we don't look at her or speak to her," Catherine said.

Heat filled Matt's chest. He opened his mouth, and Catherine placed a palm over it.

"And I informed her that we will be respectful of her request because we *choose* to and not because she's demanding it. We acknowledge she's mourning. Kim has also agreed to keep her hands and feet to herself." Catherine glared at her.

"We need to have a serious conversation when we're back," Matt said.

"No talking!" Kim stomped forward.

Catherine rolled her eyes and hurried along, side-by-side with Matt.

Not much later, they were back at camp, just on the other side of the lake. The winds in camp were stronger than in the forest they'd just crossed. Above them, the sky swirled a menacing gray. Matt stopped at the bank of the lake.

"Welcome to Camp New Beginnings." Justin splayed out his arms. "Where the weather is just as dysfunctional as its residents."

"Very funny," Catherine said. "Come on, let's get to the main hall."

"Wait." Matt pointed toward the back. "Is that another . . . crap, it is. See the funnel?"

In the southeast part of camp, a small funnel cloud twisted and dipped toward the earth, then was sucked back up into the sky, growing larger each time it plunged to the ground.

"Now what?" Stacy asked. "Back into the forest? I can't run anymore. I'm exhausted."

"Cody?" Matt asked. "You're the most experienced with tornadoes."

"Well, I'd say let's give it a few minutes." Cody held his pants as if he were cupping a belt buckle in the front. "If it touches down and stays connected to the forest floor, we're better off laying on the low edges of the lake. The forest has too much potential for shrapnel. If it keeps going up and down like that, it'll probably dissipate—"

A loud rumble of thunder sent the tornado to the ground. It twisted, then slowly migrated to the east.

Boom!

A thick column of white smoke erupted from the ground and blossomed into a mushroom cloud. Fire erupted within the explosion, igniting a small cabin. Rain poured down without warning, and the twister was sucked back up into the sky.

"What the heck?" Stacy held Darin's arm. "Tornados are like bombs now?"

"No," Matt said, shaking his head, "that's impossible."

Everyone huddled together, staring at the smoke.

"I can't believe he did it." Darin slicked his wet hair back. "That crazy old bastard. He really did it."

"You think Dr. Westbrook did this? He's dead." Matt's face twisted with confusion. "That's laughable. You can't blame everything on him."

"Bro, that was my belt." All color had drained from Darin's face. "That psycho actually strapped a live bomb onto my body."

CHAPTER 22

"I'm not doing this here," Darin said. "Let's get out of the rain."

They ran, slipping on the red, muddy pathway on their way to the main cabin. Once inside, Justin started a fire. Catherine placed seven chairs around the hearth.

"My belt. It really was a bomb," Darin said. "I mean, that's what he told me. I was worried, but I never—not really—ever thought it was really a bomb. I mean, I knew there was a chance, but I figured he was just trying to scare me."

"We can't be sure that was what exploded," Matt said. "The people who buried it are . . ."

"Nathan told me," Cody said. "I asked him where. That was the general area. I just wanted to make sure it was in a good spot. Plus, I knew it needed to be reburied. They had only buried it under the snow, not into the ground. I liked him and Victoria plenty, but they didn't have a lot of survival instincts, you know?"

"No, they didn't, did they?" Kim said. "If that stupid

goth girl had, like, any brains, my boyfriend would still be alive!"

"Kim!" Matt growled and pinched the bridge of his nose. "We'll deal with you later. For now, either zip it or go back to the stage like you were before."

Kim tried to cry but only managed to make her face red.

"It's the only thing that makes sense. The tornado picked up my belt and somehow detonated it," Darin said. "Westbrook could have killed us all."

Rain beat down hard against the roof and the south-facing windows.

"Why would he do that?" Justin asked. "He really didn't trust you. Why?"

"Because I wasn't a puppet," Darin said. "He did some things . . . I can't get into it, but there was distrust. And it wasn't on his end. He broke *my* trust. In the end, I was in a hostage situation. Forced, you know."

Matt held the exhaled loudly and started to walk off.

"Fine," Darin said. "Westbrook was eccentric when I first met him after he woke me the first time. I figured it was the isolation, plus I was only twelve. I didn't have enough life experience to realize he was completely deranged."

"Qualify that," Catherine said.

"It started off with little things that struck me as odd. Like he would count his steps as he walked. Then demand I did too. He'd make me give him my numbers throughout the day. That's what he'd call it: my numbers. If I lied, he'd actually know the correct number of steps I'd taken. Who does that? He was obsessive about everything."

"Maybe he was just bored," Matt said.

"No. It was more. Things started breaking, things that shouldn't. Like individual pods. Columns could go out, sure, but not one cryopod here and there. They were all connected. But he'd always manage to be the hero and save the day by fixing it. He was creating problems just to fix them."

"Are you positive?" Justin asked.

"It went on for years. I finally caught him one day when I was supposed to be on the other side of the cave. This was maybe a year before I was forced back into cryosleep. Which, honestly? I was thankful for. I didn't want to be a part of it and his sabotage any longer."

"No way," Matt said. "Why would he do that?"

"So he could be useful? Because he was crazy? Make himself our savior? Hell, I don't know," Darin said. "You're asking me to make sense of someone who made none."

"But you knew him. You knew him better than anyone else," Matt pleaded. "I just can't imagine this selfless man was . . . misguided."

"Did I really know him? Do we really know anyone? Westbrook was three different people. The valiant person he wanted to be—which is what you saw in the videos. The smart scientist who cleverly fashioned solutions out of his hat. But when the camera was off, he was the sick, scary man that I knew."

"The camera . . ." Matt started. "The videos."

"Wait," Catherine said, pacing. "What if Darin is right? If Dr. Westbrook truly was sick? I can't believe I'm saying this, but what if the cryopods weren't failing?"

"No, they were failing," Darin said. "I know that for

sure. They'd almost failed in the past. I saw it with my own eyes."

"Then maybe he made them malfunction?" Stacy asked.

"Yeah." Darin's eyes darted to the left, and he stared at the floor. "Maybe."

"I believe you, Lance-Darin," Stacy said.

"Why didn't you tell us all this in the beginning?" Matt asked.

Darin kept his gaze on the wooden floor. "You had this image of him already in your head, and you'd never even met him, not really. It was clear from the word go you didn't trust me. I really didn't see the point in making the rift worse."

"Yeah, well, I think I almost trust you less now." Matt crossed his arms.

"Do you believe me? About Westbrook?" Darin asked.

"If that bomb hadn't exploded, I wouldn't have believed you. I guess I kinda do," Matt admitted. "But maybe you were the bad guy, and he had to threaten you."

"If I was the villain, why wake me?" Darin asked. "If I was that big of a threat, why give me a bomb? I could have detonated it myself and collapsed the entire cryovault and killed everyone."

"I . . ." Matt trailed off. "Wait a minute . . ."

"What?" Cody asked.

"This makes more sense. On the videos, he said that you had died." Matt scratched his head. "That means he lied. You didn't die. He just put you back in cryosleep."

"Well, there you have it. I didn't die. I'm here in the flesh. And he did lie about me dying."

"What were you, captain of the debate team in high school?" Justin walked by Darin and toward the window. "You got me convinced."

"Never made it to high school," Darin said.

"Oh right." Justin shrugged.

"This is a lot to process," Matt said.

"Darin, I'm with Matt," Cody agreed. "I believe you, but it's a lot to think about."

"I don't care who believes me," Darin said. "I was there. I know. And if he was telling you that I died, and I actually didn't, then you shouldn't believe him at all. I don't know what his motives are . . . or were. All I know is that we should do all we can to survive."

More gears pounded and shuddered through Camp New Beginnings.

This time, the grinding was pure metal on metal.

"Justin, is the cabin still burnin' out there?" Cody asked, his eyes darting from side to side.

"Nope," Justin said. "Smoldering a little, but the rain mostly took care of it. Also, it's not raining anymore. But the mountain is on fire."

"What?" Matt stood so fast, his chair screeched over the wood and tipped over.

He jogged over toward the window and stood next to Justin. Atop the highest peak of the mountain, smoke plumed. A small burst sent small red debris into the air.

"That's not a fire!" Matt's voice trembled. "That a volcano, and it's about to blow!"

CHAPTER 23

Several small bursts sputtered from the mountain, followed by more smoke. The gray sky had cleared to a pale blue. But now, smoke streaked through the blue and swelled until Matt worried that soon, the sky would be entirely darkened again.

"Okay, everyone, stay calm," Matt said. "The smoke could just be steam eruptions, meaning it's not going to erupt for a while."

"How can you, like, tell the difference?" Kim asked. "You're an expert on this too?"

"I can't," Matt said. "You're right. We need to leave. Pack up what you can carry, and we'll take off."

"Where are we going?" Justin asked. "Back to the gears?"

"R&D Lab—the Sev." Matt stalked back toward their supplies on the stage. "It's on higher ground and built into the hill. I think we should be safer there."

"You think." Kim sat in a folding chair. "But you

don't know. All you do is guess and, like, get people killed."

"Kim!" Matt yelled. "If you're so unhappy with me, then don't follow me. No one is making you."

"Oh really? Then why did you drag me out of the forest? Force me to follow you?"

"Because I wasn't going to leave you to die," Matt said. "But if you want to keep fighting at every turn, then just leave me alone. I don't have the energy to fight with you anymore. Please."

Matt snagged a few lanterns, slipped on his backpack, and headed toward the door. As he palmed the door handle, the whole cabin vibrated violently.

Boom!

Matt flung the door open and ran to the edge of the deck. Giant plumes of black smoke were escaping the mountain. Small explosions within the smoke continued the momentum. It billowed higher and higher, blanketing the sky in darkness. Then covering the entirety of Camp New Beginnings.

Matt turned back to everyone in the gym. "We need to get out of the main cabin!"

Catherine screamed behind him.

Matt coughed and held his shirt over his nose. A fountain of red and orange lava erupted like a geyser. The top of the mountain burst open, allowing the column of fire to shoot straight up. Another explosion rattled the ground and sent shockwaves through the cabin.

"Get your packs!" Darin yelled.

"Let's get outta here!" Matt shouted, and grabbed Catherine's hand.

She locked eyes with him, panting, sweat dotting her brow, and nodded before running down the stairs.

The haze thickened by the minute. Matt counted six people. He inhaled acrid air that sent him into a coughing fit.

"Stay close!" Matt yelled. "We can't get separated!"

"Ah!" a female voice yelled. "I'm hit!"

"Keep going," Matt yelled. "Ahh!"

A thick piece of molten lava struck Matt on his arm. He instinctively grabbed the singed flesh, only to burn his hand and pull it back immediately.

Lava rained down at them like meteorites falling from the sky. It didn't make sense; Matt knew this wasn't how volcanos erupted.

"Help!" Stacy collapsed.

Without missing a beat, Darin picked her up.

"Stacy, are you okay?" Darin's voice was filled with genuine concern.

"No," she cried. "Please don't leave me here."

The sky was a burnt orange hue, casting them into what felt like hell to Matt. A piece of molten rock, the size of a basketball, crashed into the ground ahead of them, spitting steaming-hot dirt clods in every direction. The incoming chunk of lava left a crater three feet in diameter. The earth tremored again, and a blast sent them all tumbling to the ground.

Catherine winced and stood, holding her shoulder. She bit her lip, holding back tears. Justin pulled Cody to his feet.

"I'm burnt real bad," Cody yelled. He limped toward the lake and jumped in fully clothed.

Catherine followed suit. Everyone else joined in except Darin, who helped Stacy dip her foot in to cool it off. Even Kim swam out to the middle. Matt treaded water and stared at the mountain. It was like a scene out of a movie. Pieces of red-hot rock and lava shot down around them with intense force. A piece of liquid lava splashed into the water close to them, boiling the water as it sunk deeper. The cool water warmed rapidly.

"No," Matt said. "We're going to get trapped in here. We need to get out of the lake."

Matt swam to the edge and pulled himself out. His arm throbbed, and he smelled burnt flesh. He took note of everyone's injuries when they emerged from the lake.

Half of Catherine's hair had been singed off, and part of it was burned into her shoulder. Justin was pretty banged up, but Matt couldn't see any large burns. Stacy must have stepped on something hot enough to melt her shoe away and burn the sole of her foot. The back of Cody's thigh had a bright red mark where his pants should have been. Kim treaded water, her feathered hair swishing around her.

The sky around them reddened even deeper. Small fires broke out, blocking the path.

"Come on, Kim," Matt said. "We're not waiting. We have to go."

"No!" she screamed. "Look at you idiots. Every one of you is hurt. But not me! I'm still perfect. I'm not letting you drag me into danger. I'm safe here."

"Kim, please!" Stacy screamed. "We can't leave you."

"Scram!" Kim yelled.

A smaller piece of hot ash landed on Matt's shoulder, singeing his shirt. Sulfur steamed off the lake. Matt looked behind him.

"We're beggin' you," Cody said. "We gotta go."

"Then go!" Kim said. "How about you go—"

A high-pitched whistle zipped through the sky. Matt looked up and saw a bright orange ball careening toward the lake. Kim stared in shock. Before she could scream, the fireball smashed into the side of her face. Her skin melted, her hair burned off instantly, and her right eye became liquid and oozed down her face.

Stacy dove into the water and swam to Kim. She held Kim with one arm and swam backward with her free hand, legs kicking furiously. Lava bits cascaded down all around them, hissing the water's surface. Matt and Darin waded into the water and pulled them both to shore.

Kim's face was completely black. Her skin had melted off on point of impact, exposing her teeth like she was smiling. Her eye was gone, and her cheekbone was an open hole of charred bone. Gray brain matter leaked out of her exposed skull bone.

Stacy wailed.

Matt looked over his shoulder. The mountain released a river of lava that crept toward them.

"We don't have time for this," Matt said. "Grab your backpack! We need to move, now!"

"We can't leave her!" Stacy said.

"What choice do we have?" Catherine's voice trembled. "We can't carry her body and you."

Stacy nodded and sniffled.

Catherine quickly hugged Stacy and ran toward the

north. Away from the volcano and toward the truck and lab.

In one day, Rhett, Victoria, and Kim had died. Matt felt such guilt with Rhett and Victoria, but not with Kim. He'd begged and pleaded with her all day. Maybe she willed herself to die. Maybe Mother Nature heard her call and obliterated her head with a chunk of lava rock. It was nonsense in its own way, and he couldn't play mind games with himself now.

Now, it was time to run.

CHAPTER 24

The lava crept toward camp as the fractured group climbed the hill toward the truck. Matt's thighs burned, and his mouth tasted like acid cotton. He hoped in the deepest parts of his heart that the lava wouldn't follow the same path as the avalanche.

"Hang on," Darin said. He gingerly placed Stacy down near the mangled truck where they'd all started their journey just days ago. "I need a second. That hill was brutal."

"I'm sorry." Stacy stood on one foot and balanced herself on Darin.

"Don't be." Darin was hunched over, and his hands rested on his knees. He looked up at Stacy and smiled. "I'm just glad you're alive."

"Really?" Stacy smiled, but it was a sad smile.

"Yeah." He stood and embraced her.

Matt looked down at camp. Lava still exploded from the top of the mountain in the distance. He wondered if there was even going to be a camp to return to. He squinted to see if any of the buildings were still standing, but it was too dark.

"I guess our plans of going to the mountain are canceled," Matt said. "We should probably get going."

Catherine winced when she stood.

"I gotcha." Justin took her pack from her. "I'm thirsty."

"There's water at the lab. It's not far," Cody said.

"You never mentioned water!" Justin said. "All right!" He greedily drained his green canteen.

"Justin," Matt said, facing him, "there's an even better surprise that I think you're gonna love."

"Right on." Justin wiped his lips.

They hiked past the truck and into the field toward the hill. The little bit of light that shone through the heavy smoke faded quickly as evening took hold. Constant coughing became their theme song. Matt stopped and lit one of his lanterns. They circled the base of the small hill until they reached the metal door to the R&D lab.

"We're here." Matt pushed in the door. "Welcome to the Sev."

The thick dust caused him to cough more.

Once everyone was in, Cody quickly closed the door and shoved a handkerchief in the broken handle, sealing the smoke out.

"Wow," Darin said. "What is this place?"

"Follow me," Matt said. "To your right are the blue drums filled with water. On the opposite wall are the black barrels. We think they're hazardous based on the skull and crossbones painted on them."

"Go, go, Inspector Gadget," Stacy said.

"I used to love that cartoon," Darin said, then blushed. "It's weird that I was younger than you when we were put in cryosleep, but now I'm older than you, right? Heck, I'm old enough to drink."

"Speaking of that . . ." Cody nodded at Matt.

"Water first," Matt said. "Grab your canteens."

Cody pumped on the bright orange top, and water sputtered out at first before he got a steady stream. One by one, they filled their canteens, drank them, and came back for more. After their thirst was quenched, Matt led them through the lab and into the back offices. He showed them the food closets and saved the larger office/junk-food room for last.

"Catherine, would you like to be my assistant?" he asked.

"Sure." She tried to force out a smile. Matt worried about how badly she was hurt.

"Behind door one, I present to you"—Catherine opened the door and presented it like she was one of Bob Barker's Beauties "—chips!"

"And behind door two, we have Twinkies and Ho-Hos!" Matt unsealed the cabinet. It hissed like a soda can.

"Door three," Catherine said, "chocolate and non-chocolate candy."

"Kim would have liked that," Stacy said quietly.

"And behind door four, the coup de gras!" Matt unsealed the final heavy cabinet.

"Is that? Sweet mother, is that *beer*?" Justin stood, mouth agape.

"And cheese balls. Wanna crack the first one?" Matt tossed him a plain white aluminum can labeled "BEER" in plain, black, blocked letters.

If it had been a few days ago, Matt would have made a crack about Justin being able to read. But now, he was thankful he had a friend to lean on. He was glad they'd come this far.

Now that the adrenaline was wearing off, Matt's burned arm felt like it was boiling.

"How about we set up in here?" Matt asked. "I'll grab the packs."

"Wait, you think we're okay to have a couple of beers?" Catherine asked.

"Why not? I mean, technically, we're like forty-five or somethin'," Cody said.

"Don't feel like you have to drink one if you don't want," Matt said.

"No, I mean, you're right. We're technically of age," Catherine said.

"And who cares?" Stacy hobbled toward the cabinet and helped herself to a can. "It's not like there are any cops here to bust up this party."

"I meant, should we be celebrating? We lost so much today," Catherine said.

"It's not celebrating." Justin popped the tab on his can. "It's taking the edge off. I'm in a ton of pain. I'm sure you guys are too."

Catherine nodded.

Justin took a long drink from his can and burped. "Well, it's a little skunky, but not as bad as I figured. Glad it's not hot in here, or they'd be rank. Anyway, I think I'd like to have one before I clean out my wounds."

"That's not a bad idea," Matt said. "And I think we should eat, fix ourselves up, then we can all talk about . . . well . . . everything, I guess. It's been a hellish day. And now that we're sort of safe, I'm starting to really hurt."

Darin passed the plain white "BEER" cans around. He stood in the middle, held his up, and said, "To Kyle, Nathan, Rhett, Victoria, and Kim."

Everyone held their cans up and repeated the toast.

CHAPTER 25

Matt swallowed the last bit of beer from the can. He felt a pang of sadness. He'd never have a chance to finish his conversation with Victoria down by the dock. Or even really get to know the true her.

"That made me feel a little dizzy," Matt said to Cody.

"Me too. I ain't had one since the last branding at my daddy's ranch." Cody helped Matt sift through the contents of the backpacks, hoping for first-aid kits.

"Your parents let you drink?" Matt asked.

"Only at brandings," Cody said. "It's tradition. At the end of each branding, everyone has a Coors Original and Rocky Mountain oysters. I was only ever allowed one or two, but after bein' in the hot sun all day, and kicked by a steer here and there, it was pretty nice."

"Wow." Matt stacked a small first-aid kit onto another he'd found. "I'd never had alcohol until today."

"How's your arm feeling now?" Cody asked.

"Not as bad," Matt said.

"See? Just like Justin said, took the edge off. You findin' anything?"

Stacy's scream sent chills down Matt's spine.

"Just some basic kits. The good stuff is still at camp," Matt said. "You?"

Stacy shrieked again.

"Same. I guess let's see what we can use," Cody said. "I'll meet you in there. I'm going to double-check the cabinets in the lab."

"I hope Darin is able to get all of Stacy's shoe off. It looked like it had melted into the bottom of her foot. Pretty terrible luck, stepping on a molten lava rock like that."

"Yeah, it was pretty gruesome," Cody said. "But most of the shoe melted away. I think once he gets the edges loose, the rest will fall off."

Matt handed Cody his lantern in the lab, then followed the light emanating from the larger office.

"Hey," he said, entering the room. "We found a few things, but we'll need to head to camp tomorrow or once it's safe for the rest of our gear. Cody's checking out the lab right now for additional salves and bandages and whatnot."

Stacy lay with her head in Darin's lap. Her foot, propped up on Catherine's legs, was wrapped in a white lab coat. Blood seeped through, staining it red.

"How'd it go?" Matt asked.

"You heard," Darin said. "Did you find any pain pills?"

"No, the Lortab is still at camp," Matt said.

"Well, I'd suggest drinking a bunch of water and

downing another beer, Stacy," Justin said. "You'll at least fall asleep."

"O-okay," Stacy whimpered. "You still have to clean it out, don't you?"

"I'm sorry," Catherine said. "We do."

Stacy sat, plugged her nose, and downed several large gulps, then leaned back on Darin. "I don't remember beer being so disgusting."

Catherine carefully unwrapped Stacy's foot. The top of her foot wasn't too bad, but the bottom was raw, red, and bleeding in several spots.

"Just do it," Stacy said. She squeezed her eyes shut and held Darin's hand. "Get it over with."

Catherine placed the lab coat under Stacy's foot and poured water from her canteen over it. Stacy squirmed and cried out. She begged for Catherine to stop. Within a few seconds, it was over. Matt handed Catherine a tube of antibiotic cream from the small hiking first-aid kit he had carried in his pack.

"Stacy, I'm going to put some salve on your foot, okay? It might sting at first, but it'll help heal it and keep infection away," Catherine said. "We don't have a ton, so I'm only putting it on the open wounds, okay?"

Stacy nodded. Her face was bright red, and tear streaks cut through the dirt on her cheeks.

Matt felt a little nauseated and decided to check in with Justin instead of witnessing this. He grabbed a white canister of cheese balls and headed toward Justin, who sat with his back facing Stacy.

"How bad are your wounds?" Matt asked.

"Not too bad. I was a running back. I did pretty good

at dodging the debris. Only small burns. Lots of them, but nothing like the others got. My skinned forearms probably hurt the worst."

"You should still clean them," Matt said. "Our medicine is pretty limited back at camp."

"Do you think it'll still be there?" Justin asked.

"Camp? Or the main hall?" Matt asked.

"Either." Justin swigged his beer. "This whole thing is screwed up."

"I know." Matt removed the clear lid from his cylinder container and peeled back the silver seal. He tilted it in Justin's direction. "Cheese ball?"

"Thanks."

Justin took a handful and stuffed a few in his mouth. Matt did the same. He looked over his shoulder, and Stacy was lying on her side. Darin stroked her frizzy hair.

"How are you feeling?" Matt asked.

"I told you, I'm not too hurt," Justin answered in between bites.

"No, I know. Not that, the other thing," Matt said.

"I don't feel anything. It sucks we lost any of them, especially Rhett. He was my buddy. But I guess I figure we're all going to die soon, probably. We just have to try and delay it as long as possible."

"Yeah," Matt said.

The earsplitting sound of gears started up again. The sound encompassed them like the smoke.

The room fell silent.

"You guys hear that?" Cody burst into the room.

"Great, what's next?" Stacy cried.

"Maybe nothing," Matt said. "Maybe something.

Either way, we're in the best spot. I think we'll be safe here."

"I hope," Catherine said. "I honestly don't think I can take any more natural disasters tonight."

"You know what? Let's actually live like tonight's our last night." Matt tossed a movie theater-sized box of chocolate candy in Catherine's direction. "Normally, I say we need to ration, be smart, don't overindulge— well, don't overdo it on the beer, but everything else? Eat it. Have fun. After you clean out your wounds, though. That's a non-negotiable."

"You're serious, aren't you, chief?" Justin asked.

"Why not?" Matt passed out more candy, Ho Hos and cheese balls. "We should celebrate. We can't sit here and keep focusing on what we lost. We need to celebrate what we overcame! We survived a flash flood, a treacherous snowstorm, monster avalanches, dozens of tornados, and a volcano eruption! We *did* that! Never mind we survived the cryosleep and car crash."

Plus, it could be our last night at this rate.

"Don't forget the bomb," Darin said.

"Oh yeah!" Matt said. "Darin lived through a live bomb being strapped to him. Who's in? Huh? Who wants to have fun? Eat, drink, and be merry, and tomorrow we live. No talk of death or what-ifs or Westbrook at all."

Darin locked eyes with Matt. It was the first time Matt had referred to the scientist by his last name only. Either Darin was a great liar, or Matt was starting to see the cracks in Dr. Westbrook's façade.

"Beer me," Justin said.

CHAPTER 26

Cody didn't find any additional medical supplies in the lab. But he did find an old boom box and batteries. The silver, boxy JVC stereo had two round speakers on either side of a tape deck. Above it was the radio station feature, complete with a twist knob for manual searching. Below the tape deck were all the usual buttons—pause, fast forward, rewind, record, eject—with play and stop being the largest buttons of all.

Matt put the batteries in and hoped for the best. The gray cassette inside had a white label and blocky print that ironically read: "mix tape."

"Here goes nothing." Matt pressed the play button. It clicked, but nothing happened. "Dang."

"Let me check," Catherine said. She opened the back of the boom box. "The batteries are in backwards, Matt!"

Catherine giggled, and she replaced them. She pushed play and squinted her eyes, waiting.

Loud trumpets ripped through the silence, then Gloria Estefan's upbeat voice, followed by snappy piano.

"The conga?" Matt laughed. He laughed so hard tears streamed down his face. "My mom *loved* this song!"

"Get up!" Catherine pulled Matt to his feet and placed his hands on her waist. "Darin, help Stacy, you guys lead!"

Matt stared at Catherine's shoulder. Her hair that had melted into her skin was gone now. But it left behind a deep, blistering burn. It glistened with antibiotic salve. Despite her injury, she looked like she was ready for the club with a trendy, off-the-shoulder *Flash Dance* shirt and an edgy haircut: long on one side, short on the other. She started out reminding him of Cher, and she'd now become his Jennifer Beals.

Darin gave Stacy a piggyback ride, and Catherine held Stacy's waist. They formed a conga line like they were at a wedding reception. Kicking feet out to the side. Moving forward and back. Matt's heart ached. Every time this song came on the radio, his mom would perk up and crank up the volume. At the time, it was so embarrassing. Now he'd give anything to relive that moment. He had to find her, but he was at a complete loss as to how.

"I cannot believe those batteries worked!" Darin yelled. "This is hilarious."

Cody was the first to drop off once the music ended. A piano chord progression started the next song.

"Well, this one's a downer," Justin said. "Journey? Lame. I wonder if they got any Metallica on there."

"Leave it for a sec," Matt said, taking Catherine's hand, placing it on his shoulder, and putting his hands around her waist. The slow-tempo lyrics of "Faithfully" took him back to his first high school dance. Steve Perry belted out the mesmerizing words. Catherine put her head on his chest, and they swayed back and forth. For the moment, all worry and pain melted away, and Matt was in the now.

The song ended with full electric guitar overlaying the grand piano chords. Catherine stopped him. "Matt, are you okay?"

"I'm just, I dunno, I feel really helpless. Our parents are stuck somewhere. We're no closer to them than we were the first day."

"Hey!" Justin shoved a silver bag of potato chips at him. "What about no being sad or whatever crap you said? Here, eat your feelings."

"I'm sorry." Matt sat and took a deep breath. "I can't help it."

Darin sidled up to Stacy. Catherine trimmed the wick on the lantern and joined the rest of the group in a circle around the light.

"I'm feeling pretty bad too," Stacy said. "Lance-Darin, you've been a dream, and I'm so thankful for you. But I can't get the image"—she burst into tears—"of Kim's face exploding like that out of my head."

"Or Victoria's," Matt said. "Her head was completely cut off. I know we said we'd try to find their bodies and bury them, but I hope we never find hers. I don't want to see her like that."

"I feel awful for saying this, but I hope all the bodies are just gone when we get back," Catherine said. "They were all so, so mangled. I honestly think I've been traumatized or something."

"If we can go back," Darin said. *"If."*

"You ain't wrong about that," Cody said. "But we gotta try. Most of our stuff is still back there."

"You want to go back?" Catherine said, her voice cracking.

"No, but we gotta go back, don't we?" Matt asked.

"I can't even walk!" Stacy said. "I'm a burden."

"No, you're not." Darin put an arm around her.

"Cody is right," Matt said. "A few of us need to try tomorrow and see what we can salvage. More clothes, supplies, and first-aid stuff. But I think this bunker is our new home."

"You Shook Me All Night Long" ended, and Tiffany's one-hit wonder, "I Think We're Alone Now" blared from the speakers.

"We really are alone now." Justin sat in the corner, his head cradled in his hands. "Screw this song."

"Not for long," Matt said.

Justin looked up; his long, sandy-blond hair was matted to his right cheek.

Matt lifted his chin and said, "We're going to find the cryovault. Mark my words." He hoped he'd make good on his word.

TO BE CONTINUED

As a kid, Tyler H. Jolley always had a knack for storytelling. When he grew bored of old fables, he created his own exciting and unique worlds. Many years later, he still had so many new ideas and stories swirling in his head, but with nowhere to share it. That's when he put his pencil to paper and let the creative juices flow.

His debut novel, *Extracted*, came out in 2013 and swiftly became an Amazon Best Seller and Spencer Hill Press Best Seller. *Prodigal* and *Riven*, the second and third books in The Lost Imperials series were released in May of 2015.

After a brief hiatus he restructured and returned to writing. His Adventurous Ali series has received much praise. To date, he's released three in the series.

When he's not writing, you can find him at his orthodontic practice, mountain biking, or on the hunt for the perfect doughnut.

www.ingramcontent.com/pod-product-compliance
Lightning Source LLC
Chambersburg PA
CBHW020334110726
47898CB00003B/870